Slaughter Gang 3

Willie Slaughter

Lock Down Publications and Ca$h Presents

Slaughter Gang 3
A Novel by *Willie Slaughter*

Willie Slaughter

Lock Down Publications
P.O. Box 870494
Mesquite, Tx 75187

Visit our website @
www.lockdownpublications.com

Lock Down Publications
Like our page on Facebook: Lock Down Publications @
www.facebook.com/lockdownpublications.ldp
Cover design and layout by: **Dynasty Cover Me**
Book interior design by: **Shawn Walker**
Edited by: **Jill Alicea**

Stay Connected with Us!

Text **LOCKDOWN** to 22828 to stay up-to-date with new releases, sneak peaks, contests and more...

Thank you.

Submission Guideline.

Submit the first three chapters of your completed manuscript to ldpsubmissions@gmail.com, subject line: Your book's title. The manuscript must be in a .doc file and sent as an attachment. Document should be in Times New Roman, double spaced and in size 12 font. Also, provide your synopsis and full contact information. If sending multiple submissions, they must each be in a separate email.

Have a story but no way to send it electronically? You can still submit to LDP/Ca$h Presents. Send in the first three chapters, written or typed, of your completed manuscript to:

LDP: Submissions Dept
Po Box 870494
Mesquite, Tx 75187

DO NOT send original manuscript. Must be a duplicate.

Provide your synopsis and a cover letter containing your full contact information.

Thanks for considering LDP and Ca$h Presents.

Dedication

This book is dedicated to my loving wife, Machumu Slaughter. You've stood by my side through the rough times, and I'm thankful for you. Our struggles have led to our success.

Prologue

Renika James sat, in disbelief, on the cold, woodgrain courtroom bench. She couldn't believe the jury had found him guilty. The high-profile case of her larger than life, dope boy fiancé, Cedric Livingston, had ended in the worst possible way. After she bore witness to the look of defeat on Cedric's face and in his body language, Renika broke down in tears as the reality of what just happened settled in. Her thoughts stumbled over one another as she reminisced on what appeared to be her life falling apart before her very eyes.

Renika doubled over on the bench, crying. The district attorney had made every charge stick: the malice murders, illegal distribution of cocaine, meth, and heroin, and illegal firearms. All of that added up to the sentence of Life without Parole.

Renika had spent most of her years living with her mother, Chessica Frankfurt, living her best life. She went to the Ivy League college in Garland, Texas, where they lived, and her father made sure they never wanted for anything. Thinking about her father, Renika sat up straight on the bench. She hadn't talked to him since before hearing about him being on the run. She'd seen the news reports, reading that he was no longer a suspect concerning the unsolved murders, and with that thought, along with what she was going through, she decided to give him a call.

Renika's call went directly to voicemail. She tried to call three times, and became frustrated because she kept getting the voicemail. She sighed out of frustration, thinking of a way to get ahold of her father. She scrolled down her contacts list, looking for someone who could help her.

Renika came across Demetri's name and decided to give him a call. The phone rang twice before he answered.

"Hello? Demetri speaking," he said, answering his phone.

Renika took a deep breath to gather her thoughts. "Hi, Uncle Demetri. It's me, Renika."

"Why, hi there, young lady! How have you been?" Demetri said, sounding excited to hear from her.

"I'm not doing so great at the moment. My fiancé just got sentenced to Life without Parole," she replied.

Demetri could hear the sadness in her tone of voice. "What can I do to help you, Renika? I am pretty sure that I can pull on a few strings to change things around."

His readiness to assist her perked Renika up. "Thank you, Uncle Demetri. We'll have to discuss that some other time. Right now, I'm still inside of the courthouse."

"Your fiancé's trial was today? Why haven't you been called?" Demetri asked demandingly.

She chose her next words carefully. "Again, Uncle Demetri, I'll tell you about it later. Do you have a way to get ahold of my father?"

"Hold on, dear," said Demetri. He called a number on three-way. A woman answered.

"Good afternoon, Demetri. How may I help you?" she answered.

"Yes, it's a wonderful afternoon, Machumu. Is your husband around?" he asked.

"Yes," was her response before handing him the phone.

"Hello?" said Li'l Will as he held the phone to his right ear.

Hearing his voice, Demetri merged the calls. "Li'l Will, there's someone on the line for you."

Li'l Will frowned. "Okay. Who is it?"

10

"It's me, Dad. Renika."

Willie Slaughter

Chapter One

There was a moment of silence between them. Li'l Will's frown turned into a serious expression. "Is everything alright? Are you hurt?"

"Not physically, Dad," Renika replied.

She gave them the watered down version of what had happened, how Cedric took the charges when, in reality, he didn't have a clue what was going on.

"All he knew was, one minute we were shopping at the mall, then the next minute the feds were everywhere," she explained.

Demetri chimed in on the conversation. "So Renika, what's it going to be?"

She didn't answer right away. She thought about what she really wanted to do. "Dad, I was wondering if I could come live with you for a few months."

The silence returned. Li'l Will was in deep thought. Renika hadn't ever asked him such a question. "Of course you can, Re-Re. You're my daughter."

"Great!" Demetri butted in. "Where are you located now? I'll send my personal helicopter to pick you up shortly."

Renika texted Demetri the address where she would be located. He received the text message.

"Okay. Sending the chopper your way ASAP, young lady. Be safe and sound," Demetri said before hanging up.

The conference call was disconnected. Renika picked herself up and was headed for the exit when they brought Cedric out wearing the faded county's blue jumpsuit, handcuffed and shackled. The sight of him brought back the tears. She fought off the emotion by running out of the courthouse.

***

Li'l Will hung up the phone and handed it back to Machumu, who looked at him questioningly.

"What was that about?" she asked.

Dee and her son, Li'l Bee, Ruby, and Tasha, Li'l Will and Machumu's three-year-old daughter, sat silently at the dining room table. Li'l Will took a good look at their facial expressions and knew they were waiting for him to answer the question.

"My daughter Renika is coming to live with us for a while."

Machumu, Dee, and Ruby looked confused. It was evident they didn't know anything about Renika. His mother made it clear.

"Alrighty then, Li'l Will James," his mother began. "Who in the world is this child you're talking about? And where's her mother?"

Li'l Will shook his head, knowing he'd opened up a can of worms. "Do we have to do this now?"

"Yes," his mother said while nodding her head.

Li'l Will laughed. "Well, you all will have to wait until she gets here. And then, you can ask her."

Li'l Will pushed back the chair and left without saying another word.

Ruby looked at Machumu and said, "Child, you're a better woman than me."

Machumu frowned. "What's that supposed to mean?"

"The man has children you didn't know anything about," she replied.

Machumu shrugged her shoulders. "We all have our skeletons in the closet, Mama Ruby. They might not be children, but they're things we don't care to share with anyone."

Before Ruby could respond, Machumu got up from the dining room table and walked out. She caught up with Li'l Will, who stood outside, enjoying the weather. She kissed him on the right side of his neck.

"Alright, luv, you know that's the right spot," he said before turning around to face her. Although she didn't ask, he could tell she wanted to know the answer to the question his mother had asked.

"Maybe I'm trying to turn you on, Mr. James," Machumu said seductively.

They kissed and held each other. Li'l Will looked at the time on his Citizen timepiece. It was 1:39 p.m. In a couple hours, things would be different at the estate, he thought to himself.

***

Down in Albany, Georgia, things were on the up and up for The Slaughter Boyz. With Teddy as mayor and Mike as the sheriff of Albany and Henry as the man holding down the fort as far as the dope game went, everything was running smooth, like a well-oiled sewing machine. The crime rate was at an all-time low. But, on the dark side of it all, the dope game was a great success for the team.

Teddy was holding a public address in the town square. Mike and his deputies were on security duty around the perimeter. It was a sunny day. Everyone was out in their summer wear.

"Citizens of Albany, Georgia, as your mayor, I'm thankful to be able to stand before you today, saying the crime rate is at an all-time low! We're receiving more government funding for schools and after-school programs for the youth! The list goes on!" Mayor Teddy James exclaimed.

The people of Albany gave him a standing ovation. Some even whistled. The public address went on for another hour or so. Teddy was walking around, shaking hands and talking to the people, when his phone vibrated inside of his front pocket.

He pulled out the phone and, without looking at the caller ID, answered. "Hello? Mayor Teddy James speaking.

"Good afternoon, Mayor James," the man said.

Upon hearing the voice, Teddy already knew who he was talking to. "Mr. Demetri, what a pleasant surprise. How's the family? And how may I help you?"

Demetri laughed at the thought of him asking Teddy for help. "No service required at the moment. I was just calling to congratulate you on your success. Your team is doing a great job at keeping business running smooth."

Teddy shook an elderly man's hand. The man was attempting to say something to him, but Teddy excused himself in a polite manner, telling the man he was on an important call, and that if he had an issue that needed to be addressed, to set-up an appointment. After getting the elderly man to agree, Teddy returned to his conversation with Demetri. "Yes sir, business is greater than ever."

"I know. Well, keep up the good work, Mayor James. I'll be in touch," Demetri stated and then hung up.

Teddy put the phone back in his pocket. He walked over to where Mike and a few deputies stood. "Gentlemen?"

They nodded. Mike, realizing it was his cue to excuse himself to have a conversation with Teddy, did so. The two men walked off from everyone to have some privacy. While walking, Teddy filled him in on the phone call he'd just received from Demetri.

"So, what do you think is next, fam?" Teddy asked Mike.

Mike was staring at the back side of a 5'10", dark chocolate sister who was wearing some see-through white spandex pants and a black halter-top. Teddy followed his gaze and nodded approvingly upon seeing where his attention was focused on.

"Mike, snap out of it, fam. Bros before hoes and business before pleasure," Teddy reminded him.

Mike forced his attention away from the beautiful black woman strutting by, but not without waving at her first. She smiled at him and waved back. Once she was no longer in sight, Mike gave Teddy his undivided attention.

"Sorry about that. What's good, bro?" Mike said.

"Fam, we got this shit sold up. The whole Albany is tap-dancing to our beat. I'm just trying to figure out what's next," Teddy replied.

Mike hunched his shoulders. "The hell if I know, bro. All I can say is, we keep making this shit happen. We popping right now, so let's keep it popping."

"Word, fam. Let's clear the square so you can jump on your me time." Teddy said

Mike laughed. "You dead-ass right. I got to find out who she is."

They walked back into the swing of things. The mayor gave a closing speech, and the people went on about their business. Mike caught up with the woman he'd seen, and they stood in front of Papa John's talking. He'd found out her name was Tierra and she was thirty-three years old without children

"Why haven't I ever seen you around here before now?" Mike asked.

Tierra hunched her shoulders and kept a straight face. "Depends on what you were looking to see."

Her comment made him smile. "And you got some flavor about yourself. I should've been looking for you."

She laughed. "It's obvious you were looking in all of the wrong places, Sheriff Mike."

"Damn, you make the title sound so much better, luv. Maybe I'll hold on to it a little while longer," Mike said.

"Do that for me. You never know what rewards might come behind it." Tierra looked at the time on her watch. It was 1:28 p.m. "Excuse me, Sheriff Mike, but I have to go. I'll get up with you at a later date if you don't mind."

"Roger that, Tierra," he replied comically.

She smiled and walked away. Mike watched the sway of her hips all the way until she got in her candy apple green 600 Benz and drove off.

Chapter Two

Renika stepped out onto the top stair of the private jet. As she walked down the stairs, a million things were going through her mind. She knew she didn't have anything to worry about. Her thoughts were more about her fiancé than anyone else.

The good thing was, she didn't have to wait for a ride or catch a cab to the estate. Renika had pretty much pre-planned, knowing her father wasn't going to say no to her coming to live with him. She had sent her car ahead of time to the airport to be kept in storage. With a baggage boy tagging along behind her with her luggage, she walked over to the storage container and unlocked it.

"Would you be so kind as to slide the door open for me?" Renika asked the young man.

He set the luggage down and did as she asked. Once the door was opened, he moved to the side. Renika reached into her purse, pulled out a hundred dollar bill, and gave it to him.

"Thank you for your services," she said.

The man took the money and pocketed it. "You're welcome, ma'am. And thanks for the tip." He dapped off.

Renika hopped behind the wheel of the glossy violet 911 Porsche, sitting on low profiles and chrome six star rims. She pulled out of the container and onto the asphalt. She turned on the radio and tuned in to the local news reports. She took a left at the stop sign and got off on the first exit.

She noticed the patrol car parked on the street. She didn't think anything of it until the cop pulled behind her and flashed the lights. Renika sighed out of frustration as she pulled over to the side of the road. She knew the only reason the cop was pulling her over was that she was young, black and driving a 911 Porsche.

The short and stocky Caucasian male officer approached the back of the car and smashed the taillight on the right. He stepped around to the driver's side. He looked down through the large frame mirror tint sunglasses and wide brim hat and spat tobacco juice on the ground next to the car.

"License and registration, ma'am?" he asked in a southern drawl. Renika cooperated. He looked over the driver's license. "Ms. James, do you have any illegal substances or weapons in the car?" he asked while looking in the backseat.

"No sir," Renika politely replied.

The officer spat again. "Then you wouldn't mind if I searched the vehicle, right?"

She frowned. "I apologize, Officer, but you don't have permission to search anything of mines."

"We'll see about that, Ms. James." The officer spit tobacco juice and walked back to the squad car. He sat in the car for fifteen minutes, and then returned to Renika's car when another patrol car pulled up on the scene. The other cop got out and walked over to the passenger side door.

"Ms. James, step out of the vehicle," the younger police demanded.

"For what?" she asked. He ignored Renika and opened the door.

"I said get your ass out of the vehicle, now!" he demanded in a hostile tone.

As soon as Renika put one foot on the pavement, all hell broke loose. Two unmarked sedans pulled up and four masked men hopped out and opened fire on the police officers. They didn't have time to react to the assault. The gunmen gunned them down, jumped back in the cars, and sped away in the opposite direction. Renika casually eased her leg back inside and closed the door and drove off like nothing ever happened.

***

Nicole and Mark were living their best life. Italy proved to be the home of homes, especially with Demetri and Thaddeus only an estate over. The four of them had brunch together every day, during which they made plans for future events. Like now, Mark and Nicole were being entertained by the twins.

"Mark and Nicole, what would you two have me do for you?" Demetri asked.

Mark looked at his wife, Nicole, who had a sly grin on her face. He knew she wasn't going to give up the opportunity to get something out of her uncle.

"Well, since you put it like that, Uncle, I need my own private jet," Nicole said.

Demetri's eyes widened with surprise. "You definitely know how to ask big, Nicole."

"I'm just saying, Uncle. You asked," she replied, smiling from ear to ear. "Besides, you never know when you are going to need to fly around on business. Right, Mark?"

Mark nodded his head in agreement with his wife. Demetri and Thaddeus looked at each other. They were really trying to decide who would foot the bill. Nicole realized they were having a hard time coming to a conclusion, so she offered a solution.

"Uncles Demetri and Uncle Thaddeus, why don't you go in half and half to buy my private jet? That way, nobody feels like they didn't do their part," Nicole said.

21

Thaddeus sighed resolutely. "Seems like we've reached a conclusion. Alright, Nicole, you'll get your private jet."

Mark couldn't help but laugh. His wife definitely knew how to get her way. Not that he himself didn't respond to her the same, because he did.

"It seems like Nicole wins again," Mark said.

Nicole kissed Mark on the left side of his face. "Aww, baby, it's a natural thing for me."

They sat, talking about upcoming business that they would be summoned to handle privately. Mark and his wife listened attentively to what Demetri was saying. Everything they did for the family took perfect timing and skill. It was definitely a big step up from what Mark was accustomed to.

After everything was finalized and Nicole had proven she'd heard the details of the contract correctly, she and Mark left.

Chapter Three

Cedric was sitting in the federal holding facility, waiting to be transferred. For the most part, everyone seemed on the nice side to him, which he considered to be because of his high profile case more than his build and appearance. He was 6'3" and 215 pounds solid. Cedric always found himself sitting off to the side no matter what was going on. His first day inside the pen had taught him that. One of the guys who'd come in with him had been made as an informant of the Feds, so after the word had gotten around to the right social circle, three of the inmates shanked him up good. According to the officer, he didn't survive through the night.

The lifespan of a rat, Cedric thought to himself while looking at CNN. There was a breaking news report, reporting the shooting deaths of two on-duty deputies. No leads in the case. He was so into the story that he would've missed chow call if it wasn't for the brother who always lagged around until everyone else was gone.

"Say, li'l homie, it's chow call. Trust me, you ain't going to miss shit. That's CNN. Same shit on repeat around the clock," the man said.

Cedric got up off the stainless steel bench that provided little to no comfort. "Good looking, bro," he said, thanking the man.

"My nigga, we're locked up. If we can't look out for each other, who else do we think going to do it?" the man replied before extending his right hand in Cedric's direction. "I'm Montana."

Cedric took hold of his hand with a firm grip. "The name is Cedric, but you can call me Ced."

"That's what's up, my nigga. Let's get this grub before we be eating out of the box tonight. A nigga getting money, but ain't no need of turning down shit they got to offer," Montana said.

Cedric nodded. "I feel you, bro. Let's go."

Montana and Cedric walked out of the cellblock together. They made small talk about sports and politics on the way to the chow hall. While they waited in line to get their trays, they kept quiet and focused their attention on the environment. It was known to go down at chow call, especially at the morning and last meal.

The line moved quickly. Montana and Cedric picked a table in the corner by the wall to eat at. It was the third Wednesday of the month, so it was fried chicken, biscuits, mashed potatoes with gravy, pound cake, and sweet tea for dinner.

"So, what's your story, my nigga?" asked Montana between bites.

"I got caught down bad with the work, bro," Cedric replied.

Montana finished eating the piece of chicken he was working on. "You don't look like a dope boy, my nigga." He said and looked up at Cedric. "Matter of fact, you look square as hell, but looks can trick a nigga."

Cedric laughed. "On the real, I'm a college graduate, had a lot of shit going for myself. Not to mention, I was engaged before this bullshit came up."

Montana raised his right eyebrow. "In other words, you took the fall for your bitch."

"No, it wasn't like that, bro," Cedric shot back quickly.

A smirk spread across Montana's face. He'd heard it all before. "It's all good, my nigga. You ain't the first, and definitely won't be the last to take the rap for his bitch. I just hope she's a Bonnie about the situation."

"Hell yeah," Cedric said confidently.

"How much time you looking at?" Asked Montana.

"At least a dub," Cedric answered and started back on his meal.

Montana almost choked on the chicken. He drank half of his tea to wash the chicken down. "My nigga, who got you sprung like that?"

"Renika James," Cedric said happily.

Montana was dumbfounded. "Do you know her parents?"

"I got to meet her mother," Cedric replied. He looked up at Montana and could see the uneasiness within his posture. "Are you alright, bro?"

"Yeah, I'm good, my nigga," Montana said. He got up from the table. "Listen, li'l homie, I'll catch up with you back in the dorm."

"Alright, bro," Cedric said without looking up from the tray before him.

Montana took his tray to the tray window and left the chow hall. On his way to the dorm, he stopped and told the guard in the booth that he needed to speak with the superintendent immediately. The guard eyed him nonchalantly as he picked up the cordless phone and called up front. He relayed the message and waited for the response, which we came, the guard ended the call.

"Go on up, front inmate. Mr. Cartwright is waiting on you," the guard said.

Montana didn't respond, not even to tell him thank you. He hurried up front, where the superintendent met him outside of his office. Montana's paranoia outlined his presence.

"Is everything okay with you, inmate?" Cartwright said, laughing. It was always humorous to see the so-called hardcore inmates under pressure.

Montana slid off into the office and remained standing. "Why do I feel like I've been set up?" Montana asked nervously.

Cartwright stepped back into his office and closed the door. He was really getting a kick out of seeing Montana sweat. "What's the problem, Montana? You look like you've stepped in a litter of cat shit."

"Man, y'all set me up. Li'l Will's future fucking son-in -law is in the dorm with me," he said coldly.

The superintendent took a seat behind his desk and hunched his shoulders in an I-don't-care gesture. "And? It's obvious he don't know who you are or what you've done. My advice to you is, keep it that way because your ass ain't getting any special treatment."

"So, it's like that, huh? Y'all use a nigga and send his ass to the cleaner," Montana said bitterly.

Cartwright waved him off. "Inmate, you can take your scary ass back down the hallway."

Montana wanted to snap back, but he knew better. He'd heard stories of how Cartwright got down. Piss him off, and he would piss and shit on you, Montana recalled an inmate telling him when he'd asked about Cartwright. "You're right, Mr. Cartwright, he can't know. If he did, I'd be on the slab by now."

"Exactly, Montana. Now leave my office," he demanded.

Montana opened the door and left. What the superintendent said made a lot of sense, however, not enough sense to make him comfortable, he thought while walking back to the dorm. Just so happened when the officer in the booth popped the door for him and he walked in, Cedric was on the wall phone. That didn't make the situation any better to Montana.

He let the door slam shut behind him. His thoughts were running wild and his eyes darted from left to right while he walked across the day room floor. Montana went inside of his cell, put the window flap up, and locked the door. He laid flat on his stomach on the floor next to the foot of the bunk and reached with his right hand to the rear corner.

Montana retrieved the shank he had hidden under his bunk and concealed it in the waistline of his trouser under his shirt. Feeling a lot more on the safe side, he popped his door open. To his surprise, Cedric was standing at his door about to knock.

"What's up, my nigga? Everything good at the crib?" Montana asked.

"Yeah, bro, everything is looking good. My lawyer filed my appeal. He said I have a good chance to knock off 5 to 10 years," Cedric replied.

"That's what's up, li'l homie. Did you talk to your wifey?" asked Montana.

"Briefly, but yeah. She's taking it kind of hard," Cedric said.

"Look at the bright side, my nigga, you got a rider on your team," Montana said. He was looking for any flaw within Cedric's movement or speech, but there was none. The tension he'd been feeling started to dissolve.

"Yeah, I'm blessed in that department, bro. On the serious tip, I was just checking up on you, making sure you were good," Cedric said honestly.

"Most definitely, li'l homie. What you about to get into?" asked Montana.

Cedric shook his head. "Nothing really. Probably about to watch a little more news and take my ass to bed. Why? What's up?"

"Ain't nothing up, my nigga. I'm about to take it in for the night myself. I'm going to leave my door rigged, so if you need something, you can get it. I got a line too, my nigga, so you can stop spending money on that high price-ass wall phone," Montana said.

"Appreciate the love, fam," Cedric replied.

"We all hood, li'l homie. I'll leave the line and charger behind the books on the table. Just bring it back to me in the morning," he said.

"Alright, bro. Have a good one," Cedric said and walked off.

Montana watched him walk over and sat down in front of the news television. He quickly rigged his door and put everything exactly where he said he would before laying it down to get some sleep.

Cedric sat, watching CNN for a good thirty minutes before getting back on the wall phone - at least, that's what he appeared to be doing to everyone else. The day room was almost empty. He and two other men remained.

Cedric stood near the entrance door, waiting for shift change. He looked at the time on his Fossil watch. It was 9:15 p.m., and, when he looked up, the cocoa butter brown-skinned, 5'4" and thick in all of the right places female guard came walking down the hallway, carrying her lunch, paperwork, and mail. She smiled and blew him a kiss as she walked by.

Cedric walked over to the table where the other two guys sat playing dominoes. He sat down on the stool facing the booth and he remained quiet. The man on his right kicked him on the foot to get his attention. Cedric reached beneath the table and grabbed the butcher's knife from him.

"You can't go in playing, young brother. That fool in there might be a rat, but he ain't a bitch by far," the bald-headed heavyset black man on his left said.

"Neither am I, big bro. Just make sure I can get away with this shit," Cedric replied.

"You good, li'l homie. Ain't nobody going to miss a fucking cheese eater. Trust me," he reassured him. The door opened to the booth, and the second shift guard walked out with his see through carry bag. "Alright, li'l homie, it's about to be show time. You ready?"

Cedric nodded. The baldheaded man signaled for his domino partner to get on point. The other man got up from the table and walked over to Montana's cell door with his ID card in his right hand, ready to slip the lock.

"You got one shot at this, youngster. Don't fuck it up," he said while listening for the door up the hallway to close. Finally, the clicking sound that the door made was heard. "Go eat, li'l nigga."

Cedric jumped up from the table and crept over to Montana's cell door. By the time he got there, the man had slipped the lock for him to walk right on in. Montana was sound asleep when Cedric stabbed him in the jugular vein twice before he could even open his eyes. He stabbed him four more times before casually walking out of the cell.

His adrenaline still rushing, Cedric walked back over to the table where the baldheaded man sat and sat down on his right side. "He's as good as fucked, big bro," Cedric said while handing him back the butcher's knife under the table.

He took the blade and wrapped it up inside of yesterday's newspaper. He stood up, walked over to the door, and pressed the intercom button to get the guard's attention. She opened the door immediately, and he walked out of the dorm, over to the booth drawer, and dropped the newspaper inside after she slid the drawer out for him. Without exchanging words, he walked back in the dorm and sat back down at the table.

"Young blood, you forgot a very important principle," he said.

Cedric was confused. "What's up?"

"The spoils belongs to the victor, li'l nigga. Go get that line and whatever else in there of value. I'm pretty sure a dead man ain't calling anybody or eating food," he replied.

Cedric nodded and jumped up from the table. "Understood, big bro." He went back inside of Montana's cell and took everything of use. The three of them divided up the spoil, however, they told him to keep the phone because they already had their own. After they finished, they locked down in their individual cells and went to sleep like nothing had happened.

Before Cedric could get too deep in sleep, the guard buzzed the speaker in his cell. He rolled over onto his back and stared at the speaker.

"Cedric Livingston, what's up, boo? What are you doing?" she asked seductively.

"I'm living. What's on your mental, Tiffany?" he replied.

"Some release therapy. Come to the booth. Just stay ducked down when you come out of the dorm door," Tiffany said.

"On the way, sexy," he said and got out of bed. Cedric opened his cell door and made his way across the day room floor to the front door.

Tiffany popped the door for him, and he did exactly as she'd said. He stayed low to the floor until he reached the booth door, which she had cracked open for him to slide inside. He immediately noticed she was already out of her pants and panties. "Damn, baby girl, you was already plotting the moment huh?"

Tiffany sat up on the control panel, spread her legs wide, exposing her freshly-shaved vagina, and leaned back against the window of the booth. "Something like that. Are you going to please this pussy or what?"

He responded by walking up in between her thighs and dropping his pants and boxers to the floor. Tiffany was already soaking wet, so he slid inside of her with ease. She gasped for air as his stimulating length filled her and his lips pressed against hers hungrily. She worked her hips, grinding on him and moaning softly in between kisses.

"Oh baby, give me that dick. I want it all, baby," Tiffany whispered in his right ear between moans.

Cedric, feeling his release coming, grabbed her by the thighs and started long stroking inside of her hard and fast, causing her to moan louder and louder. She wrapped her arms about his neck, holding on to him and thrusting herself into his pounding inside of her.

"Cum in me, baby. Cum inside of this pussy, baby," Tiffany said softly in his ear.

Cedric pounded away hard and fast until he came. The release was so strong it caused his legs to tremble. Tiffany held on to him tight and grinded on him, milking him dry and climaxing herself. Satisfied, they tongued each other down while waiting on their bodies to calm from the release.

"Damn, Tiffany, you know how to make a nigga get right," Cedric said while pulling up his boxers and pants.

Tiffany giggled. She wiped herself with the wipes she had in her bag before putting on her panties and pants. "So you say, boo. Time will tell though."

He didn't quite understand what she meant by that, but he kissed her again before creeping back into the cellblock. Instead of jumping in the shower, he washed off in the sink in his cell. While at it, his thoughts were on the powerful release he'd just felt. He knew if Tiffany wasn't on the pill, shots, or IUD, there was a chance that was the nut to get her pregnant.

Cedric took a piss and laid down with the thoughts of Tiffany being pregnant. *What will I tell Renika?* he thought to himself. "Oh well," he said out loud. With that thought lingering in his mind, sleep claimed him quicker than he thought it would.

Chapter Four

The next morning, he awakened to Tiffany's voice coming through the speaker in his room, telling him good morning and that she would see him later on. He asked her for her phone number, which she gave him without hesitation. He promised to call her around dinner time.

"Okay, boo. My relief is coming down the hall. Talk to you later," Tiffany said and turned off the intercom.

Cedric had plans on going to breakfast, but found himself going back to sleep. When he did wake up, he already knew he'd missed breakfast because everybody else in the cellblock was up and about. He got on up, used the bathroom, washed his hands, brushed his teeth, and washed his face. On his way out of his cell, he grabbed a honeybun out of his box.

Cedric sat down in front of the television news, eating the honeybun. Although watching CNN, his attention was really on the conversation some of the guys were having about Montana being found dead after shift change this morning. *Damn, she put that pussy on me good last night*, Cedric thought to himself. It was the only logical conclusion he could come up with for not hearing the officers and nurses come in and take Montana's corpse out on the gurney.

The brother who had slipped the lock for him last night came walking over and sat down next to him on the bench. He handed Cedric a small, folded piece of paper. "Here you go, young blood. You're going to need this."

Cedric took the piece of paper and immediately stuffed it in his right sock. "What's that?" asked Cedric.

"SIM card for your line, li'l homie. I'll let you call and activate it when I pull out after lunch," the guy replied.

"That's love, big homie," Cedric said and pounded him up.

"You play bones, li'l homie?" he asked Cedric.

"Yeah, bro. What's up? You want to play a few games?" Cedric said.

"Come on. Let's see what you got, youngster," he replied.

They left from in front of the television and sat down at the domino table, where the baldheaded man was already waiting for them.

"By the way, my name is James Slaughter. And that's my brother, DeQuan Slaughter," James said, introducing himself and his brother.

"It's a pleasure meeting y'all. My name is Cedric Livingston."

The three men talked while playing dominoes. Neither one of them spoke of what had happened the night before. James even knew Cedric had fucked Tiffany, but the pen had its rules. The code of silence was the golden rule amongst the rules behind the wall.

***

Dink was doing what he knew best, checking trap. Bumping "Ghetto Dope", he drove from the east side of Albany to the west in his brand new Cadillac Seville collecting dues. Although the murder rate had been at an all-time low, the few murders that did occur were his doing. Taking shorts on his money was the one thing he couldn't come to terms with, and everybody knew it.

Dink pulled up in front of Trav's trap house and hopped out. Fiends were coming and going, so he knew business was good. He swaggered up to the porch and took a seat, waiting for Trav to come back outside.

He rolled and fired up a blunt of sticky green while he waited on his right hand man to finish serving his customers. A fiend, who couldn't have been older than twenty-two, walked up on the porch. She was a 5'9" redhead who was pale, but still had a little shape about herself. The perfect example of what Dink considered a functional junkie.

Instead of knocking on the door and walking in, she sat in the chair next to him. "Can I smoke with you?" she asked.

Dink damn near choked to death on the smoke trying to respond. "No disrespect, but I don't know where ya mouth been. You know how y'all get when it comes to wanting that blow," Dink replied.

She sucked her teeth. "First of all, I don't suck on glass dicks. I only snort a line of coke every now and then to take the edge off a fucked up life away. Secondly, I don't care for sucking dicks either. And my name is Mindy."

Dink pulled out his stash of marijuana and a White Owl blunt and handed it to her. "Roll your own problems."

Mindy busted the blunt down with her thumb nails and dumped the tobacco out. She broke down three big buds of the sticky green and spread it across the length of the blunt. Dink watched as she twisted and licked the blunt to make it stick. The way she wrapped her moist lips around it had his mind on exploring her sexuality.

"What?" asked Mindy. She pretty much knew what he was thinking: the same as every other man thought when it came to a woman.

Dink hit his blunt hard. He held in the smoke for a few seconds before exhaling. "You already know what's on a

nigga mind, Mindy. We ain't going to role-play this conversation out. I'm Dink."

Mindy laughed and fired up the blunt of sticky green.
"Are you married or in a relationship with someone else?"

He puffed on the blunt again while the memory of his
ex-wife haunted him. She had grown tired of hearing about
all of the street drama he was always in, so she'd taken the
children and dipped to Tulsa, Oklahoma, where her mother
and father lived. It wasn't a week later that she'd sent the
divorce papers through the mail with a letter informing him
she would make arrangements for him to see his children
twice a month. Since then, he'd been playing the field.

"No and no. I'm very single. Used to be married. My
wife jumped ship on a nigga," Dink said.

Mindy hit the blunt and nodded her head in deep
thought. "Damn. Sorry to hear that, but I'm not the hit it
and quit it type."

"Who said anything about a one night stand?" asked
Dink.

Mindy took another puff and smiled. "We might be on
to something then, Dink. What's your number?"

"Let me see your phone?" he asked.

Mindy handed him her phone. Dink created a contact
with his number and name, and then gave it back. She stood
and walked off the porch.

"Where you headed?" asked Dink.

"To work. I'm good now. Some good green is as good
as a line. I'll be in touch," she said without stopping or turning around.

Dink watched her walk to the curb and jump behind the
wheel of a glossy red Mitsubishi Eclipse sitting on chrome
five stars and low profile tires. *I know the bitch ain't broke*

looking for a come-up, he thought to himself as she drove off.

Travis finally came limping out of the house onto the front porch behind three customers. He plopped down in the chair next to Dink and accepted the blunt Dink held out to him. "What's up, fam?" asked Travis.

"You know me, my nigga, bill collecting for the next drop. What you got for me?" Dink said.

Travis just so happened to look up the street and saw his little nephew down by the courts. "I got everything needed, fam. Excuse me for a minute." He limped down the porch steps and out to the curb. "Li'l Tony, bring your li'l bad ass here! I know you hear me!"

Li'l Tony came running up the street. Travis waited on the curb. Once he got to him, Travis limped back up onto the porch and sat back down.

"Boy, why your li'l bad ass ain't in school? Lie to me, I'm going to embarrass ya ass in front of company," Travis said coldly.

Li'l Tony stood before his uncle and Dink on the porch. He didn't want the ass cutting Travis was ready to give him, so lying wasn't an option. "I ain't going to lie to you, Unc, I got suspended last week for fucking a broad in the bathroom during lunch break. Mama don't know about it either."

Dink busted out laughing. "Dammit, man! You can't be mad at the li'l nigga for that!"

"Nah, but he know what time it is. Don't you?" Travis said.

Li'l Tony nodded his head. "Yes sir. Stay in school, go to college, and become somebody other than just another nigga on the block slanging dope in the hood."

"Fucking right," said Travis. "Now take your bad ass in the house. I'm not going to tell your mama, but your li'l ass going to work while you're around here. Understood?"

"Yeah, Unc, I understand," said Tony before walking inside.

"Don't be sneaking drinking up my Ciroc either!" Travis yelled.

Dink continued to laugh. "I like that li'l nigga, fam. He just doing the same shit we used to do back in the days."

"Yeah, but this ain't back in the days, fam. Cops killing young innocent black children on the regular. Especially young black men. I ain't trying to have my nephew become another statistic. Hold on." Travis stepped into the house.

Dink thought about what his right hand man had just said. It was reality. Cops were killing young brothers on routine stops every other day in different states. The cruelty of the reality had him mad, and he was definitely thinking about having something done about it.

"Here you go, fam. Dink?" Travis said nudging him on the shoulder with the duffle bag. "You alright, my nigga?"

Dink stood up and grabbed the duffle bag. "I'm good, fam. Just thinking about the shit you said a minute ago. That's some real deep shit, my nigga. How much is this?"

"$75,000, fam," Travis replied.

"You be on it, bro. I appreciate ya. We'll get up later on. Probably hit The Fox since it's Friday." Dink said while walking off the porch. He walked to his car, got in, and drove off, still thinking about what he wanted to do.

***

T and Henry were at the studio with a couple of new artists. To Henry, they sounded good. But T wasn't feeling their vibe. He cut the music off and turned on the booth intercom. "Say, young gangstas, y'all got to spice that shit up. The lyrics on point, but y'all niggas ain't putting out enough emotion with this shit. Take that shit from the top," T demanded and turned the track on again.

Henry had twisted a blunt and fired up while T was giving orders. He bobbed his head to the funky track the two new artists were rapping to. "Yo, T, that shit really dope," Henry said

"Yeah, they alright, Li'l Henry, but the sound quality ain't hitting on shit. That's the problem," T said.

"When did you become the music scholar?" asked Henry.

"The day I decided to do this shit, fam. It ain't rocket science. All it take is an old soul and some good ears to know the difference between quality and bullshit." T looked through the booth at the artists. "See, that's the bullshit." He turned off the track and turned on the loudspeaker. "Get the fuck out of my studio."

The two young men threw their hands up in a "what's up" gesture.

"I said, get the fuck out of my studio! Don't make me repeat myself!" T said demandingly.

Reluctantly, they took off the booth headphones, grabbed their gear, and walked out of the booth. Passing by T and Henry, one of the artists made a smart remark under his breath that T heard clearly.

"What the fuck you mumbling for, li'l nigga? Something wrong with your vocal cords?" T said in a not so polite way.

"Nah, fool, I'm good. Are you?" he replied.

Hearing the sarcasm in his voice, T jumped up and caught him with a three piece snack, two quick jabs and a left hook to the jaw, sending the artist down to the carpeted floor. "When y'all young niggas going to learn not to pop off at ya mouth if you ain't ready to pop off for real?" T said as he started stomping him out.

Henry continued to smoke. He didn't move to stop T, however, he kept a watchful eye on the other man. Finally, T quit stomping the young man. He gestured for his partner to help him up.

"Take your scary ass partner and kick rocks," T said angrily.

They left without exchanging words with T.

"What's wrong with this generation?" asked T as he sat down next to Henry. "They ain't built for shit, but they got a lot of mouth."

Henry simply nodded in agreement while inhaling the chronic smoke. They chilled and smoked three more blunts at the studio before deciding to leave.

Chapter Five

Sopia was living her best life. Her restaurant was the hottest spot in town. Every now and then Mike would come through to check on her, but her girl Tanya made her cut that visit off. They had grown strong, and Sopia was cool with meeting whatever demands she made.

Matter of fact, Sopia had made Tanya the manager. The two had moved in together in a nice ranch style four bedroom house by the lake. Since they weren't worried about having company or thinking about adopting children, they turned one of the extra bedrooms into a gym, another into a Jacuzzi room, and the third one into an office. The office was Tanya's idea because she enjoyed keeping up with their finances and she loved doing research and writing poetry.

It was 3:26 p.m. Everything was starting to wind down. Although owner and manager, Sopia and Tanya still did their part, whether it was helping to cook or washing dishes. They normally closed at 4:30, however, they would stick around inspecting the dining, prepping, and cooking areas before leaving. Usually, that would keep them busy until around 6:40 because they inspected each area like a real inspector.

That was another one of Tanya's ideas. She would always remind Sopia about being safe rather than sorry. The dining area had cleared, and the kitchen help were gathering the dirty dishes off of the tables. After washing and towel drying the dishes and utensils, Sopia told them they could go ahead and leave for the day, that she and Tanya would handle putting everything up and lock up for the evening.

With everyone gone except for them, Sopia and Tanya put the dishes and utensils away, inspected each area, and retired to their office inside of the restaurant for a while. Sopia looked at the clock on the wall. It was 6:39 p.m.

"Tanya, what's up, boo? How you feeling?" asked Sopia.

Tanya, who always dressed in body dresses and heels, sat on top of the office desk in front of her. "Sopia, why you ask a question you already know the answer to?" She eased her dress up, revealing she had no panties on, and slid the straps off of her shoulders and took her bra off.

Sopia stood licking her lips while taking in the flawless dark chocolate body before her. Every time she looked at Tanya's exposed sex and blemish-free naked body always seemed like the first time, Sopia thought to herself.

"What are you waiting for, boo? Come make love to me," Tanya demanded while spreading her legs.

Sopia closed the distance between them quickly. She immediately went face first between Tanya's thighs, licking, thrusting her tongue inside of her and sucking on her clitoris. Tanya moaned and rubbed the crown and back of Sopia's head. "Mmm, Sopia, baby... Yes, baby... Yes... Make love to me," she demanded.

Sopia responded to her demands by thrusting her tongue deeper and sucking harder on her clitoris, which caused Tanya to thrust her hips forward as the orgasm claimed her body. After Tanya's fruity tasting juices flowed around her tongue, Sopia stood up straight and undressed herself. Tanya smiled and leaned back on the desk, gesturing with her finger for Sopia to climb on top of her, and she did.

They tongued kissed and lip locked in between moans while Sopia slid her body up and down gently on top of

Tanya's. Their breast and sexes pressed hard against each other, and their clitorises rubbed every time Sopia slid up and down.

"Oh, baby... I love making love to you, Tanya. Mmm, baby. I'm about to cum, baby," Sopia whispered softly into her left ear.

Tanya began grinding with her hips. As she felt Sopia's body began to tremble, she held her firmly against her body. Sopia slid up and down on top of her faster and faster, moaning uncontrollably in her ear, until she came.

"Damn, baby, I can't get enough of you," Sopia said, breathing hard.

Tanya held on to her trembling body and kissed her on the cheek. "I love you too, boo. Come on, get up, so we can go home. Round two is on me when we get there."

Sopia got up and got dressed. Tanya didn't bother putting her bra back on. She pulled the straps back over her shoulders and stood up and pulled the dress back down to cover her exposed sex. Sopia couldn't help but look at her lustfully.

They locked up the restaurant and walked hand in hand out to the glossy money green drop-top Mustang. Tanya hopped behind the wheel, leaving Sopia to get in on the passenger side. "You must knew I didn't feel like driving?" Sopia said.

"I know my wifey," Tanya replied as she put the car in gear and drove off.

It was 8:18 p.m. when they made it home. Tanya kept to her word. She sexed Sopia in the shower and in the bed before they laid down to sleep.

***

Dinner was almost ready to be served at the estate. Li'l Will and his family sat around the dining room table. His mother, Ruby, was talking about taking the children to church on Saturday and Sunday. Dee had agreed to go along with them.

Li'l Will straight up declined going. He knew from all of the dirt he'd done and was still doing that he was beyond saving. Machumu declined the invitation as well, reminding them she was Jehovah's Witness. That left Ruby and her grandchildren and Dee.

"Y'all need to get ya lives right with the Lord," Ruby said.

"Mama Ruby, you got to remember, everybody serves God differently," Machumu said in response to her comment.

Li'l Will held his head in his hands and sighed, knowing his wife had just opened up an argument. And sure enough, his mother didn't let Machumu's reply slide.

"Now hold on a minute, young lady. Jesus Christ is Lord of lords and King of kings," Ruby said confidently.

Li'l Will peeped at his wife through his fingers. He was shaking his head, trying to tell her to leave well enough alone, but she looked him off, turning all of her attention to his mother.

"Mama Ruby, I believe in Jesus Christ too. The difference between what I believe and what you believe is how you choose to understand what you're reading. I do my own research. I don't go by another man's interpretation," Machumu said defensively.

"Child, you must be possessed with an evil spirit. Satan, get thee behind me!" Ruby yelled.

Machumu was about to respond when feminine laughter sounded through the air. Everybody's attention went to the open doorway, where Renika stood laughing at the scene.

"Hey, everybody," Renika said.

Ruby stood up and walked over to where she stood and hugged her. "Aww, look at my grandbaby all grown up and looking good."

Renika hugged her back. "I'm good, Grandma." She sniffed the air. "What's for dinner? Did you do the cooking, Grandma?"

"Nah, but I definitely gave them the recipe," Ruby replied.

If Li'l Will was ever glad to see his daughter, he was at the moment. She was like an angel coming to rescue him from a religious debate. He got up from the table and hugged his daughter. "Renika James, thank you for showing up on time," he whispered into her ear.

"I don't know, Pops. Maybe I should've stayed quiet a little longer. It would've been interesting to see who would win the debate," Renika said. She looked over his shoulder at Dee and her son, Machumu and their daughter. "I see you've added an addition to the family."

Li'l Will turned around and looked in the direction Renika was looking. "Renika, meet my wife, Machumu, your little sister, Dee, and your little cousin Li'l Bee. Everybody, meet my oldest daughter, Renika James."

They spoke to each other. Li'l Will asked his daughter to have a seat at the table. Instead of choosing a seat close to everyone, she chose to sit at the other end of the table, facing her father. No one objected to her choice of seats.

"Nice place you have here, Pops. Not quite as nice as Mama's mansion, but it's straight," Renika commented dryly.

Thankfully, the kitchen help came through with the food when they did because Li'l Will could sense a verbal war about to begin between his daughter and wife. The aroma of the different meats, sweet potato pies and vegetables gave off was intoxicating. The table was set and everyone except for the children served their own food.

"So, how's life been treating you Renika?" asked Li'l Will.

She took a bite off of the baked barbeque boneless pork chop. "Mmm. This is delicious. Grandma, you got to give me the recipe."

Li'l Will was getting a little annoyed. "Renika, I damn well know you hear me talking to you."

"Of course I do, Pops. Life been interesting for me. I have my own clothing line that's doing great, my fiancé is serving a bid for something he had no knowledge of, and the deputies down in the great state of Texas just broke my right taillight," Renika replied. She looked Machumu in the eyes. "But I can guarantee you they won't be breaking another taillight."

"Alright, Renika, that's enough. And we don't discuss certain things in the company of children," Li'l Will said warningly.

"Wasn't I the unlucky one?" she responded sarcastically.

Li'l Will dropped the conversation because he knew his daughter was trying to pick a fight. They ate the rest of their meal in silence. Once done, Renika excused herself to finish unpacking and to take a nap. After she walked out, everyone else's attention went straight to Li'l Will.

"What?" Li'l Will barked out of frustration.

Nobody said anything.

"Renika James is good people. She's just spoiled. Y'all got to warm up to her," he said.

"Spare the rod, you spoil the child," his mother stated. Li'l Will, not in the mood for a biblical lecture from his mother, left the dining room. He grabbed the stash of marijuana that he kept hidden inside of a shoe box and an Optimo blunt and stepped outside on the front porch. He sat in the wicker chair and rolled up a fat blunt without breaking up the buds. He fired up and choked on the first pull.

"Too much for you, old man." Machumu said, standing in the doorway. She had been watching him since he sat down. She walked out onto the porch and took a seat in the chair beside him. "Why you never said anything about your daughter?"

He knew that was coming. "Some things are best left unknown," he replied before hitting the blunt twice.

"But she's your daughter, Willie James," Machumu shot back.

By her calling him by his full name, Li'l Will knew she was in her feelings about the situation. "Machumu, that girl ain't no damn saint. She's probably buried more bodies than both of us put together."

"I didn't say she was. All I'm saying is, she needs to be a little more respectful."

Li'l Will chuckled in between coughs from too much smoke entering his lungs at one time. "What you see is what you get with Renika. She's about family and as loyal as they come."

"That explains her comment about the deputies," Machumu said.

Li'l Will hit the blunt again and ducked it out. "Something like that, baby. That was probably Renika's personal crew's doing. She don't go anywhere without her personal escort."

"Where in the hell are they then?" asked Machumu.

Li'l Will hunched his shoulders. "Hell if I know. No one knows until they cross her. Then, it's too late."

Machumu nodded silently. Although she resented some of Renika's ways, the picture being painted of her was that she was to be respected. She grabbed her husband by the hand. "Come on, baby. All of this tension in the air got me horny."

Li'l Will allowed her to pull him to his feet and lead him through the house to their bedroom. Inside, with the bedroom door closed and locked, she undressed him and then herself. They stood naked at the foot of the bed, kissing and roaming around each other's body with their hands. As his fingers found their way between her thighs, she gasped when he lightly pinched her clitoris.

"Man, I love the way you make my body respond to your touch," she said softly.

Li'l Will playfully pushed her back onto the bed. Machumu laid back on the bed. Her eyes were filled with lust. He climbed on top of her and kissed his way down to her sex.

Li'l Will moaned while he furiously kissed, licked, and sucked on her clitoris. She spread her legs wider and wider as the sensation continued to build inside. She grabbed the back of his head and grinded herself against his tongue and lips. She fucked his face faster and faster until she came.

Li'l Will stood back up at the foot of the bed. "Turn that ass around here girl." He demanded.

"Yes, daddy," she replied and assumed the position.

Machumu slid to the edge of the foot of the bed in doggy style. Li'l Will parted her legs and entered her from behind. Once all the way up in her, he placed his right hand at the small of her back to keep her chocolate, plump, and round booty tooted up, and grabbed hold of her left thigh with his left hand and went to work.

"Oh shit, baby! Yeah! Yeah! Give me that dick!" Machumu screamed.

Li'l Will pounded away with long hard strokes. "Yeah. You like that, girl? You like the way I'm handling this pussy?" He switched gears, hitting it from the back hard and fast at an angle.

"Oh, hell yeah, baby! Fuck me! Oh shit!" she screamed as her body shook violently from the orgasm.

He continued to lay the dick down. The wetter she became the harder and faster he stroked. "Damn, baby, this pussy good. I'm about to cum, baby." His strokes got shorter and shorter.

Machumu, feeling his sex starting to swell and pulsate inside of her, threw herself back against him. "Ahhh, shit, baby," Li'l Will said as he filled her up from behind. His strokes became a grind against her soft chocolate skin. She moved to his rhythm until he'd gone limp inside of her.

Machumu eased herself off of him and laid down on her back. He climbed in the bed beside her and kissed her on the cheek. "You're the best."

She didn't respond. Machumu continued to stare up at the ceiling in deep thought.

Li'l Will propped himself where he could look at her face. Before he could get his thoughts in order to say what was on his mind, his wife had closed her eyelids, and he could hear a light snore coming from her. He laid back down and rolled over onto his side facing the opposite direction. Once Machumu knew he'd gotten comfortable, she opened her eyes and continued to contemplate.

Chapter Six

Sarah and her daughter Tanji were enjoying the view overlooking the lake at her home. It was a cool night out, but that only added to the enjoyment. They sipped on Long Island iced tea and ate snow crab smothered in melted butter and cheese. Sarah had made inquiry about Damien, whom she knew her daughter was in love with.

"Mama, I'm going to marry him," Tanji replied.

Sarah smiled. "Of course you are, Tanji. Just don't think you're going to change the way the man makes his money."

Tanji took a sip of her drink through the straw. The liquid felt almost as good going down as the breeze coming off the lake. "Likewise, Mama. He keep on saying he don't want me working in the field or any other job if it is left up to him. But you know I'm not a lay around kind of woman."

"True. The hell with all that though. Just make sure your mother gets an invite," Sarah said.

They laughed. Working for the federal government had proven to be profitable for them with the unaccounted for currency they'd pocketed from raids, the drugs they'd replenished the streets with, and the extra they made by handling inside business for Demetri when called on. That was the biggest of their profits.

"Yeah, Italy, here I come," Tanji said.

"Correction. Here we come, baby girl," replied Sarah.

Tanji turned to the side in the beach chair to face her mother. "What do you have planned?"

Sarah sipped the Long Island iced tea. "I'm retiring, girl. Didn't I tell you after that last lick we hit it was over with?" asked Sarah.

Tanji relaxed back in the chair. She sipped the drink and looked out over the lake. "Fine with me."

Sarah didn't respond. She allowed the quietness to bring that much more tranquility to the scene. Tanji appreciated the silence. It gave her the time she needed to mull through her thoughts of when to give Damien the response to him asking her to marry him.

***

Demetri and Thaddeus were out on the shooting range doing a little target practicing. Instead of using firearms, they had compound composite long bows - Expedition Xcentric bows, to be exact. Their targets were seventy yards out.

Thaddeus drew back the coil with the razor tip arrow in place and let it fly. The arrow flew silently through the air and found its destination within the hay made target. "I'm on my A game today, bro!" Thaddeus exclaimed, resting the bow against his thigh.

Demetri smiled. "I see." He concentrated, drawing back the coil with the arrow in place. "If assassins were keener to the use of such magnificent killing machines..."He released the coil, shooting the arrow in the direction of his target. It buried itself in the target. "There would be less attention drawn to business."

They walked over to where the targets were. Thaddeus's arrow had struck inches from the bullseye, but Demetri's was dead center. Thaddeus slapped his twin brother on the shoulder. "Great shot!" he said.

Demetri nodded. He was about to respond when he heard the sound of twigs and dry leaves crackling. Quickly, he grabbed the arrow that was sticking in the hay and readied his shot. "Stay low to the ground, Thad. It makes you a harder target to hit."

Thaddeus crouched down before grabbing the arrow he'd shot. "What's going on?" he whispered. "Just stay down and be quiet. Someone's out there," Demetri whispered back. He motioned for his brother to follow his lead. Taking precaution, they ducked behind the targets, keeping the woods in view.

Three armed and masked figures stepped to the edge of the tree line. When they started talking to each other, Demetri and Thaddeus automatically knew they were Turks. As quietly as he could, Demetri took his cell phone out and texted his nephew and niece, who responded by texting they were on the way and for them to stay put. He texted back "OK" and put his phone back in the casing on his belt.

"The cavalry should be here in a short moment," Demetri said at a whisper.

Thaddeus sighed heavenward. "I'm glad they decided to live in Italy," Thaddeus whispered thankfully.

The three armed and masked figures were contemplating whether or not to approach the targets. Although they outmanned and outgunned their enemies, the Turks were hesitant because they knew the two men they'd been trailing weren't everyday ordinary men. They were made men, and killers on top of that. One of them suggested that they just shoot through the targets, so if they were hiding behind them, the shots would flush them out.

Demetri didn't know Turkish, however, Thaddeus knew enough to understand what had been suggested. "Well, brother, the cavalry need to get their asses here real quick, or we're in some real trouble," Thaddeus whispered.

"What are you talking about? What are they saying?" asked Demetri.

"They're debating on whether or not they should just shoot up the targets, hoping it will flush us out if we are behind them." Thaddeus replied.

"We are behind them. Fuck." Demetri swore in a hushed tone.

At that moment three gunshots broke the sound barrier. Demetri and Thaddeus watched as the bullets tore through the hay target next to them. 'I see they reached a conclusion," Demetri said sarcastically.

Thaddeus was thinking of a contingency plan that would save their lives long enough for Damien and Nicole to get there. "We got to lay flat on the ground. Now," he commanded.

As soon as they did, bullets tore through the hay over their heads. Demetri felt his phone vibrating on against his right thigh. He took it out of its case and read the unread text message notification. He opened his messages and sighed with relief.

"Have no fear, brother. Our saviors have arrived," Demetri whispered while putting the phone back in the case.

The three armed and masked figures became anxious. They stepped on out into the clearing with their automatic assault rifles aimed at the targets. Their anxiousness became their downfall. While they were hunting Demetri and Thaddeus, they were being hunted themselves.

Damien, Nicole, and Mark crept up from behind fast. Before going in for the kill, Damien had demanded that at least one of the Turks be left alive for interrogation. Nicole had suggested that her target would be the one. They carried razor sharp L.L. Bean Outdoors Hybrid Hunter Knives.

The Turks were talking loudly, confident that they were about to complete their mission, when things went sour.

Damien, with track running speed and expert agility, sliced through the back of his opponent's right calf with the first cutting maneuver, and with the second move, thrust the blade straight up through the bottom of the man's chin. He snatched the blade out, causing blood to squirt from the gaping wound. He was dead before his body hit the ground.

The other armed and masked men didn't have time to react. Nicole and Mark were already on them. Mark kept it old fashioned. He stabbed the man repeatedly in the lower spine and slit his throat as the man's legs gave.

Nicole's task, on the other hand, wasn't so simple, but it was simple to her. She sliced the wrist of the man's trigger hand, causing him to drop the AK-47. Afterwards, she squared off with the unarmed man. He cussed at her in Turkish before taking a wild swing at her.

Nicole blocked the unorthodox swing and countered with an open palm strike to the ribs, which she followed up with an elbow to his left jaw. The man's knees buckled and he fell awkwardly to the ground unconscious. Damien looked at his sister with a childish smirk on his face. "Showoff."

She bowed gracefully. "Why, thank you, Damien."

"Enough of the compliments already," Demetri said as he and Thaddeus came out of hiding. He stood, towering over the last living Turk. "Who do we have here?"

Damien and Mark yanked the man to his feet and held him by the arms. Nicole snatched the mask off of his head. Demetri looked at the man, whose expression showed pure hatred. "Who are you? Who are you working for?"

The man spat blood in Demetri's face before saying something in Turkish. Damien slapped him across the face.

"What did he say, Damien?" Demetri asked.

"He said he's not telling you anything. That he would rather die before he told the enemy of his people anything," Damien said.

Demetri laughed sinisterly. "Oh, is that so? You're going to tell me everything I need and want to know before you die. Tie him up and bring him along. I don't care if he walks or you can drag his ass the distance. It is the decision of whoever's watching him."

"Well, in that case," said Nicole before she judo chopped the man in the back of the neck, rendering him unconscious, "I'll enjoy dragging him."

Nobody objected to her decision. Mark and Damien took the belts off of the dead men and used them to bind the Turks hands and feet. Nicole grabbed the loop of the belt around his ankles and started dragging the man back through the woods. Thaddeus's expression was one that showed he wasn't quite understanding the psychology of his niece.

Mark rested his left hand on Thaddeus's right shoulder. "Look at the bright side of it, Uncle Thad. She's your niece, and not your wife."

"You got a good point, Mark," he replied.

Demetri and Damien laughed. "Let's get home. After a good meal, it's interrogating time," Demetri said in a sinister way.

They caught up with Nicole as she was exiting the other side of the woods near Demetri and Thaddeus's estate. The four men carried on in casual conversation, doing their best to keep from voicing their opinions to Nicole about the way she dragged the man. Once they made it to the front doorsteps, she let go of the belt loop. "Now you men can figure out who's going to carry the heavy bastard inside," she said and walked inside ahead of them.

Their prisoner groaned from the pain he was feeling. Damien grabbed hold of the belt tied around his hands and Mark grabbed hold of the belt tied around his ankles. They lifted him up like a hog on a spit and carried him in the house down into the basement, where they tied him down to a steel chair that sat in the middle of the room. They walked back upstairs and washed their hands before joining Demetri, Thaddeus, and Nicole in the dining room.

The maids brought in personal-size fruit platters and a family-size platter of pastries. Nobody said a word while they ate. It wasn't until after the maids returned with wineglasses and wine, poured it, and left that Demetri spoke.

"We are grateful for you being on time in such a critical situation," Demetri said, thanking Damien, Nicole and Mark.

"No pressure. That's what family is for," Damien replied.

Mark raised his glass in salute, agreeing with Damien's reply. Nicole tossed a grape in the air and caught it in her mouth.

"Nicole, is there something you wanted to say?" asked Thaddeus.

She tossed another grape the same way. "When will I be receiving my private jet?"

"Arrangements have been made, Nicole," he replied.

"Good," she said, getting up from the table. "Now, let's get this interrogation over with. I'm starving to try the technique I've thought of."

Demetri stared into his niece's eyes from across the table. "Out of curiosity, Nicole, when did you think of this interrogation technique?"

"Oh, just a couple minutes ago. You can never have enough ways to extract information from an unwilling source," she replied before exiting the dining room, heading for the basement.

Demetri, Thaddeus, Mark, and Damien fell in step behind her. Her brother was anxious to see what his sister had in mind. Whatever it was, he knew Nicole enough to know it would be effective. She would get the information needed and wanted from the Turk.

Nicole flipped the light switch on in the basement. Tools of all sorts lined the walls on racks. The man struggled against his restraints upon seeing her. She smiled at him.

"We're about to become best friends whether you know it or not," she said assuredly. She looked around the room for the tools she had in mind. She pushed an empty cart around the room, collecting what she considered to be her interrogation kit.

Demetri and the others looked on in silence. Even her captive had become curious of his fate in the hands of such a beautiful and well-composed killer. They watched her place a blowtorch, metal scraps, a flathead screwdriver, and a welder on the cart and rolled it over next to the Turk. She took out the L.L. Bean Outdoors Hybrid Hunter Knife and cut the man's shirt off of him and his pants legs up to just above the knees.

"This is going to be interesting." Damien thought out loud while watching his sister grab a power surge extension cord and plug in all of her gadgets that needed electrical power.

With everything set in place, she turned to her audience and asked, "Who's asking the questions?"

Thaddeus, being the levelheaded one of the twins, stepped forward. "I'll ask the questions. Just tell me when."

Nicole switched on the welder machine. "Whenever you're ready, Uncle Thaddeus."

Thaddeus crouched down to be at eye level with the Turk. "What's your name?"

The man responded by spitting on the basement floor, which was a nonverbal way of saying he wasn't talking. Thaddeus sighed. "Listen, my man, I'm trying to spare you a lot of pain. You can answer my questions in between screams from being tortured, or you can respond in a peacefully manner. Last chance. What's your name?"

The prisoner mean mugged him and spat on the floor again.

"Very well." Thaddeus stood up straight. "He's all yours, Nicole."

"With pleasure." Nicole put on the heavy duty welder's gloves. She picked up a piece of scrap metal and surveyed the size of it and set it back on the cart. "This should do the trick. Somebody hold him still please. I got to make sure I get a good weld here. Damien?"

Damien bore down on the man's shoulders with a firm grip. Nicole picked up the piece of scrap metal again and grabbed the welding gun. Without warning, she placed the scrap metal on the Turk's bare arm and began welding it in place. He screamed at the top of his lungs in pain.

"My name is Oman Jharez! Ahhhhh!" he yelled.

Nicole stop welding, but the smell of scorched flesh was undeniable in the closed-in area. Thankfully, no one was a stranger to its stench.

Thaddeus nodded approvingly. "Hmm. Nice tactic." He stood, towering over the man. "Okay, Oman Jharez. Who are you working for? And let's try to skip the spitting and screaming parts of this conversation, because I don't like being disrespected or screamed at. As you can see, my niece doesn't either."

The prisoner spoke in a harsh manner in his native tongue. What he said caused Damien to laugh. Thaddeus sighed. "I'm glad we have bilingual family members. What did he say Damien?"

"In American terminology, he just told you to go fuck yourself," Damien replied.

Thaddeus nodded to his niece and stepped back. She put down the welding gun and picked up the blowtorch and ignited the flame. Nicole grabbed the handle of the flathead screwdriver and held the head of it inside of the flame until it was red hot. She cut off the blowtorch and placed it back on the cart with the rest of the tools before turning towards the Turk, holding the flathead screwdriver where he could see how hot it was.

"This is going to be a very painful experience, Oman Jharez." She slowly pried off the piece of scrap metal she'd welded onto his arm, causing him to scream louder than he did the first time.

"I work for Dominica Citur! Get this crazy woman away from me!" Oman yelled.

Thaddeus frowned. "Never heard of a Dominica Citur. Have you, Demetri?"

Demetri sighed. It was like the past had come to haunt him after all. "Yes, I know who Dominica Citur is."

All eyes went to Demetri, who massaged his temples with his forefingers. The Turk laughed. It was a painful laugh, but he laughed. "Are you going to enlighten your comrades, Demetri Ci-"

Demetri slapped Oman across the face before he could complete the question.

"Nicole, make sure Oman Jharez here suffer dearly before he dies. I want to be able to hear his screams and cries for mercy from the wine bar, where I and the rest of the fine gentlemen will be waiting on you once you're done," Demetri said. He turned and started up the stairs. Damien, Thaddeus, and Mark were hot on his heels. They'd seen enough torture for the day, was their thoughts.

Once Nicole heard the door of the basement slam shut, she turned to Oman and smiled. "Now, where were we, Mr. Jharez?" She picked up a large piece of scrap metal, large enough to cover over half of his back. "Let's see if I can make my own version of an ironman without you dying on me." She slid the piece of scrap metal in between the back of the chair and his back before picking up the welding gun and turning it on.

Oman flinched as the fire got close to his back. Since he knew death was inevitable for him, he decided to tell his torturer what information he did know if she was willing to listen. "Hold on! Wait! Nicole, isn't it?"

Nicole walked around to face him. "Yes, that's my name. You have a last breath request?"

"I know you're going to kill me anyway, but at least allow me to tell you what your uncle won't. He's keeping dangerous secrets," Oman said.

Nicole sat the welding gun down and pulled up a chair and sat before him. "I'm sold. Talk to me, Oman Jharez."

"Before I do, promise me two things. One, you'll kill me quickly. And two, you'll do your own research on what I'm about to tell you," he demanded.

Nicole's curiosity got the best of her. For some reason, she believed the Turk was being genuine. "You have my word on both, Oman. Now, what's the big secret?"

61

"Dominica Citur is a woman. Born half Turk and Italian right here in this estate before the Turk and Italian wars. Her maiden name is Dominica Sylvan, the daughter of Charles and Havenna Sylvan," Oman said before Nicole cut him off.

"Okay Oman, this is getting to be a long drawn out history lesson. I hated history in school," she said.

"Dominica Citur is the wife of Demetri Citur, who you know as Demetri Citural." Oman stated with confidence.

Nicole frowned. "Hold on a minute. So, you're telling me that my Uncle Demetri's last name is Citur instead of Citural?"

Oman laughed, but maintained a serious expression. "What I'm telling you is, your uncle, Demetri, spawned a web of lies to cover-up generations of an identity. His wife's father, Charles Sylvan, was the true Head of the Table. Back then, it wasn't even called The Head. It was Valaire Perfecto."

"I'm following you, Oman. So, Dominica Citur is actually my auntie? Where would I be able to find her?" Nicole said.

"Reach into my front right pocket. You'll find my phone. In it, there's a contact by the name of Valaire Perfecto. That's Dominica's number," Oman replied.

Nicole reached inside of his pocket, and sure enough, there was a miniature size touchscreen cell phone inside. She pulled it out. "What's - "

"Code 2712," he said before she could ask.

"Thanks." She typed in the code. The home screen popped up instantly. Nicole didn't waste time scrolling through the list of contacts. She typed in the contact name he'd given her, and it popped up on the screen.

"I'm about to call this number, Oman. For the sake of your word, let's hope you're being informative." She pressed the call sign on the phone. After the third ring, someone answered. It was a woman.

"Hello. Is this Oman?" the woman said, sounding cautious.

"Unfortunately, no. Is this Dominica Citur speaking?" Nicole said in a casual tone of voice.

The woman didn't answer right away. "Yes, I'm Dominica Citur. May I ask, who's this I'm speaking with?"

"Of course, where's my manners? Aunty Dominica Citur, I'm Nicole Citural - well, Nicole Carter now that I'm married," Nicole replied.

Dominica laughed. "You're the niece of my husband, Demetri Citur, who changed the family name to Citural after he betrayed my father."

"Huh?" asked Nicole.

"Silly child, you're caught up in something you haven't a clue about. Let me guess. Demetri told you the bullshit story about the Turks invading, killing off some of your ancestors, and taking over the estate. Does that sound about right, Nicole?" Dominica said.

"Either you're a great guesser, or you know what you know. I have Oman Jharez right here. He's still alive at the moment," Nicole said.

"Expendable," she replied coldly.

"Is there some way we could meet? I have a lot of questions for you, Aunty Dominica," Nicole said.

"There's a GPS tracking device within the phone you're on. Keep it. I'll upload the exact location an hour from now." Dominica hung up.

Nicole put the miniature size touchscreen cellphone inside of her front left pants pocket. "You know, Oman Jharez, I really would like to let you go."

"I'm no stranger to death, Nicole. Do what you must, but don't forget to find out the truth before you continue down the path you're traveling." Oman said.

Nicole went to the corner of the basement, where a wood chipper sat attached to a duct that led outside. She turned it on. "Scream as loud as you can, begging for mercy," she commanded him while untying him.

"Why are you doing this?" asked Oman.

Nicole cut the belts from around his ankles and wrists. "Consider it an act of good faith. Besides, I know I won't be seeing you again unless it's when I meet Dominica Citur."

Oman stood to his feet and bowed gracefully. "I owe you my life, young lady."

Nicole laughed. "Who told you to stop screaming? I'm about to let you out through the tunnel. Once inside, it's a straight shot to the main road. I'm pretty sure you have a vehicle somewhere."

Still screaming, Oman nodded his head to indicate that she was correct. She located the trap door and opened it. She beckoned for him to hurry. Screaming, Oman ran through the tunnel.

Nicole locked the door back and turned off the chipper. She grabbed the sprayer and started spraying water into the chipper like it needed to be rinsed. After twenty minutes passed and she felt like Oman had made it to his checkpoint, she went upstairs to join the others. When she sat down beside her brother at the wine bar, the conversation the men were having ceased.

"A glass of sherry, please," Nicole said politely to the bartender. After the bartender poured her drink and left, she downed the sherry and swerved around on the stool and rested her back against the bar. "Oh. I'm not privy to your conversation?"

"It's not that, Nicole," Thaddeus said.

Nicole asked for another glass of sherry, which the bartender obliged her with. Without hesitation, she downed it and sat the wineglass down on the bar top. "Then what is it, Uncle Thaddeus?" she asked.

Not wanting to be the bearer of the news of a collective decision, Thaddeus nudged Damien in the side. He cut his eye at his uncle and shook his head in disbelief.

"Sis, you need to reevaluate your psych. Your intentions are great and greatly appreciated, however, your methods are kinda unnerving," Damien said.

Nicole burst into laughter. She slapped her brother on the shoulder playfully. "Don't worry, bro. I know this wasn't your idea. It couldn't have been. Anyway, I'm perfectly fine. But, for the sake of everyone else's conscience," she said, looking at Mark and her uncles. "I won't be the interrogator anymore. Matter of fact, I'm taking a vacation within my home." She got up. "Uncles Demetri and Thaddeus, I'll be waiting on my private jet too."

Nicole stormed out of the room without waiting on a response or asking Mark to join her.

"I told you we should have left well enough alone," Damien said, frustrated.

"Damien, did you not hear the way that Turk was screaming? She literally tortured the poor man to death and probably fed him through the chipper while still alive," Thaddeus said.

"So what? Didn't he try to kill you?" asked Damien.

Thaddeus was about to open his mouth to respond, but the reality of what his nephew said hit him hard. The four men sat quietly, enjoying their choice of wine.

Mark was the first to bail, saying he'd best be turning it in for the evening before he be the next person they hear screaming and begging for mercy. Although they all laughed, everybody knew what Mark said could very well become true at any moment.

Chapter Seven

Renika was sound asleep when her phone kept ringing. Tired of hearing it ring, she rolled over and answered it. Hello? And who the fuck is this calling my phone at 2:26 in the morning?" she said, looking at the time on the phone.

"Damn, Ne-Ne, don't be so uptight. It's me, Cedric," the caller replied.

"Hi hon," she said, softening her tone of voice.

"Much better. How's everything going?" Cedric said.

Renika stretched and yawned. "I have no complaints other than missing you, baby. Whose phone are you on?"

"Mines."

"Well, try calling me at a more suitable time," Renika said and then hung up. She turned her phone off, put it on the night lamp stand, and rolled back over. She was sound asleep within seconds.

***

Cedric tossed the phone on the bed and pressed the intercom button inside of his cell.

"Yes, Mr. Livingston?" Tiffany answered.

"Is the coast clear?" asked Cedric.

"Uh huh. Come on to mommy, daddy," she said seductively and popped his cell door.

Barefooted and wearing nothing other than his boxers, Cedric crept out of the dorm and into the booth. Tiffany was already out of the bottom half of her clothes when he got there. She looked him up and down, biting on her lower lip.

"I see you came prepared, baby," she said as she walked around to stand behind the chair. "Have a seat, boo," she said while patting the backrest of the leather padded chair.

Cedric sat down and relaxed. He watched Tiffany's juicy booty bounce and tremble as she walked around to face him. She unbutton her shirt and unfastened her bra, revealing a perfect set of medium-sized breasts with the prettiest nipples he'd ever laid eyes on. She dropped down on her knees and massaged his manhood through the opening of the boxer shorts.

"Enjoy yourself, my king." Tiffany said before wrapping her lips around his exposed sex. She bobbed up and down the length of him while jerking him off in a twisting motion. Her hot and wet mouth felt so good his toes started curling up.

"Dammit, Tiffany," he moaned. "Baby, you know how to please your king. Suck this dick, baby. Suck this dick."

Tiffany obliged him. She came all the way up to the head of his penis and playfully licked the top where the opening is, causing him to bear down on the arms of the chair and moan her name sexually. Feeling his sex grow stiffer, she stop and stood up straight.

"Are you ready for the ride of your life, baby boy?" she said seductively.

"Tiffany, I'm ready for everything you have to offer me," he replied.

Tiffany mounted him, setting her legs up on the arms of the chair. She slow grinded on top of him while they kissed. But as she became wetter, she started bouncing up and down on him hard and fast.

"Ooh, baby," she moaned softly into his ear. She came quickly, and the heat and wetness was more than Cedric could take.

He grabbed hold of her shoulders and started thrusting up inside of her hard and fast. "Tiffany. Tiffany. Oh shit." He moaned and groaned as he felt his release coming. "Yes, daddy, fuck me. Harder! Harder!" Tiffany yelled. Cedric's thrusts became harder and faster. The feel of her soft flesh bouncing up and down on top of him and the sound of her sloppy wet pussy was all the motivation he needed to cum.

"Mmm..." His body trembled as he came inside of her. Tiffany placed lustful and longing kisses upon his lips while grinding slowly to milk him of his release. "Baby, I love you," she said in between moans and kisses.

"I love you too, Tiffany," he responded without hesitation.

With that, Tiffany worked and pumped her hips, slapping her ass against his thighs hard and fast until they both came again. They kissed and cuddled for a while before she got up off his lap. "Alright, bae, you got to get back in before one of my coworkers comes asking me if I need a break," she said and kissed him softly on the lips.

Cedric sat and watched Tiffany wipe off and get dressed. She was a perfect match to him. He got up, and on his way out, he kissed her and told her he would call her when her shift was over. He eased on back into the dorm and into his cell, and laid it down, too tired to take a bird bath in the sink.

***

Morning came and breakfast was being served. Dee, Ruby, and the children were on their way out to church. They'd skipped breakfast on account of Ruby reminding them they shouldn't think about living on bread and water alone, but to be filled with the word of God. Besides that speech, she told them they would be serving a meal at the church.

Ruby and the others bumped into Renika in the hallway. She asked her granddaughter if she would like to join them in going to praise the Lord. Renika shook her head and said, "I'm past saving, Grandma. Take those who still have a soul."

Renika walked on into the dining room, where Li'l Will and Machumu were already eating their breakfast. She said good morning to them and sat at the opposite end of the dining table. The kitchen helpers brought her a plate of waffles, Sunnyside eggs, bacon, and her choice of orange or apple juice. She ate in silence.

Machumu, done eating her breakfast, finished drinking her glass of juice. She looked down the table at her husband's oldest daughter and smiled. "So Renika, what do you like doing for fun?"

Renika forked a piece of bacon and devoured it before answering. "Depends on mood and company. Why you ask? Don't tell me you're trying to play mommy, because that is out of the window." She went back to work on her breakfast.

"No, I wouldn't ever try to take the place of your mother. I'm just seeing where we might be able to meet on common grounds. You know, to get out of the house for a while, doing womanlike things." Machumu replied. The conversation was already exhausting to her.

Renika nodded. "Well, let's see, Machumu. I enjoy doing bad things to people who are bad for business. Other than that, I have my own personal hairstylist, massage therapist, nails doer, etcetera. All the above I like doing by myself."

Machumu set up straight in the chair, staring at Renika in disbelief. She was nothing like her father in personality. "Are you really so self-absorbed?"

Renika downed the glasses of orange and apple juice right behind each other to wash down the waffles, eggs, and bacon. "I'm a loner. I don't play well with others, Machumu." She looked over at Li'l Will. "I thought my pops would've given you the heads up by now."

Frustrated, Machumu slid the chair back and stood to her feet. "I can't with you, Renika," she said as calmly as possible.

Renika's nonchalant expression faded into seriousness. "You can't what with me, exactly? Play family? I thought I made myself perfectly clear that shit wasn't happening. My mother's still alive and doing damn great," she replied coldly.

"Renika James!" Li'l Will exclaimed, jumping up out of his seat. "What the hell is your damn problem?"

Renika remained sitting, well composed in her mannerism. "I don't have a problem, Pops. I came here to spend some time with my father, thinking maybe I would view you a little different than I've been the past eighteen years. But that's not happening."

"What's that supposed to mean?" asked Li'l Will.

Renika stood up. "Here you are, a big family man. Another child and a wife. I apologize if it seems too complex for you to understand that you not giving me the time of day that you're giving your daughter and wife might be overwhelming to my mental."

That statement hit home with Li'l Will. He could see clearly what her temper was about. The crazy part was, he didn't have a sound response to offer her. "Just calm down,

Renika. Let's talk about this," he said, his voice full of emotion.

Renika had a smirk on her face. "Maybe eighteen years ago I would've been glad to listen to what you got to say. But not eighteen years later, Pops. Matter of fact, I'm gone."

He looked at her, confused by her statement. "What are you trying to say, Renika? Go ahead and tell me how fucked up of a father I've been to you and all of the berating shit you can think of if it'll make you feel better. But you know I've provided for you since you were born."

She laughed hysterically and threw her hands up in the air. "Money can't buy or excuse a missing parent! I would've rather had you in my life, at all of my graduations and proms, than your fucking money!"

He started to say something, but she cut him off. "My bags are already packed in the trunk of my car. I'm gone. Peace out." She threw up the peace sign with both hands. She walked out with her head held high, not wanting to hear another word her father had to say.

"Well, aren't you going to redeem yourself? She got all the right in the world to be pissed off at you," Machumu said.

Li'l Will walked out of the dining room, heading for the front door with Machumu hot on his heels. When he flung the front door open, he paused, seeing Renika's crew posted on the hoods of their rides with automatic and semiautomatic assault rifles and pistols on display. Machumu looked over his shoulder and ducked back behind the door. "Shit!" she yelled before she knew it.

Renika heard her and turned around, but she wasn't in sight. However, her father was. She cracked a smile and said, "Well, family guy, I'll see you around. Maybe I will call every now and then to check up on you. I'll be sure to tell my mother you said hi." She hopped in her car and drove off, followed by her crew.

Li'l Will watched them go. Machumu came outside and wrapped her arms around her husband from behind and said, "Baby, she'll come around in her own time. She's just angry right now." Her phone vibrated in her pocket. She let go of Li'l Will and answered. "Hello?"

"Good morning, my friend. How are you doing?" the caller said.

Machumu knew Demetri's voice from anywhere. "What's going on, Demetri? How's life in Italy?"

"Oh, I don't know. Just been shot at. Other than that, I have no complaints," he replied.

"Sounds adventurous. What can I do for you?" she said.

"Well, I was trying to call Renika, but I keep getting her voicemail. Would you happen to know where she is?" Demetri said.

"Hold on." She handed the phone to Li'l Will. "It's Demetri."

Li'l Will sighed and grabbed the phone. "Li'l Will speaking. What can I do for you?"

"Why isn't my niece answering her phone?" asked Demetri, getting straight to the point.

Li'l Will already knew this was coming, and he wanted to do everything he could to sidestep it. But it was upon him, and he had to answer for his circumstance. "Well, Demetri, she stormed out of here with no intentions of coming back, if that gives you any clue of why she's not answering her phone."

There was a moment of silence. Li'l Will wasn't certain of meaning when it came to Demetri's way of thinking.

"I see. I guess we have you to thank for her sudden mood swing," Demetri said with a hint of sarcasm in his voice. "Oh well. Before I hang up, I must tell you that Montana is no longer with us. He committed suicide a couple days ago. At least, that's what the report says."

Before Li'l Will could say anything, Demetri hung up. Li'l Will sighed while handing the phone back to Machumu. "That didn't go over too well." H said.

"All this gloomy shit ain't flying around me, baby. Pep your ass up. It ain't the end of the world," Machumu said demandingly.

"Yeah, I know. But it damn sure feel like it," he replied while looking across the lawn. It was always a beautiful sight to take in. The trees, shrubs, and grass stayed freshly manicured, making things look so alive.

Machumu realized her husband was not coming off of his guilt trip at the moment. She wasn't about to stick around to watch him drown in his sorrow either. "Listen, baby, I'm about to leave your depressed ass alone for the day. Ain't nobody got time to have your life draining energy rub off on them today. I'll be back."

Machumu walked down the front porch steps and over to the four door parking garage. Li'l Will watched as she pulled out, driving her dark purple Mercedes Benz Jeep.

***

Cedric woke up to pounding on his cell door. It never failed; after a night with Tiffany, he would sleep like a baby. The banging continued until he answered. "Yeah! Quit banging on my fucking door!" he yelled.

"Young blood, get your ass up. It's breakfast call," the man outside the door said.

Cedric knew the voice. It was James. He jumped up out of the bunk, gargled some mouthwash, and splashed some cool water on his face. James banged on the door again. "Bring your ass on, youngster." He walked back over to the front door, making sure it didn't close because once it did, the guard on shift wasn't opening it again.

Cedric hurried up and put on his pants before popping out of his cell with his shirt slung over his shoulder. He bent down and tied up his Reebok Classics before putting his shirt on and catching the door. "Appreciate that, OG," he said to James on the way out.

James could smell the perfume on him. "Young G, you been doing your thang lately."

All he could do was smile. "Yeah, something like that, OG. Shit is getting real between us."

James laughed. "Alright my nigga. As long as you keep your business straight, you'll be alright."

They walked into the dining hall and fell in at the back of the line.

James's brother DeQuan was already sitting at a table along the back wall, eating. They got their trays and made a beeline for the table he sat at alone. DeQuan said good morning to them as they sat down.

Nobody said anything while they ate. It was Saturday, so breakfast was griddlecakes, eggs, chicken links, and milk. DeQuan waited on his brother and Cedric to finish eating. After they were done, the three of them got up and left together.

Back in the cellblock, they sat down at the domino table. DeQuan sneezed.

"Bless you, big bro." Cedric said, but DeQuan continued to sneeze. "You alright?" he asked.

James chuckled. "Hell no. All that perfume and pussy scent you wearing. Man, go scrub your ass."

DeQuan finally stop sneezing. He looked at Cedric and shook his head. "You're fucking up, young player. But your business is your business," DeQuan said.

Cedric didn't have a clue of what he meant. He walked on to his cell, grabbed his soap, towels, and boxers, and went to the shower.

James's phone vibrated on his thigh. He pulled it out and held it under the table. There was an incoming call from a private number. He knew it could only be one person, so he excused himself and walked to his cell.

"Talk to me," James said, answering the phone.

"What's going on inside the pen these days?" the caller said.

"What's going on, Li'l Willie? How are you holding up out there?" asked James.

"Business is good as usual, Uncle James. I heard about the move. I appreciate that love, family," Li'l Will said.

"No problem, Nephew. The li'l nigga proved to have some heart about himself, however, he ain't Slaughter Boy material. How my sister Ruby doing?" James said.

"She's living her best life, Uncle James. Right now, she's at church. How's Uncle DeQuan?"

"That nigga out there at the domino table, waiting on me. Make sure you tell li'l sis I asked about her," James said. He peeped out of the cell window, making sure the guards weren't making any rounds inside of the cellblock.

"Will do, Unc. Make sure you tell Uncle DeQuan I said love, fam," Li'l Will said. He logged into his Jpay account and transferred funds into his uncles' trust accounts. "Fam, I just hit y'all up with $300 apiece on the books. That should hold y'all over for a couple weeks."

"That's love, G. We appreciate you. Never think any different, Li'l Willie." James peeped out of the window again.

"Alright, Unc, I'm about to let you get back to your domino game. Y'all get at me whenever y'all need something," Li'l Will said.

"That's what's up, G. Hell, we'll be up out of here soon. Seven more months," James reminded him.

"Man, I had forgot. Keep me posted, Unc," Li'l Will said and then hung up.

James stashed the phone back inside of the homemade pocket on the inside of his pants before walking back out to the domino table, where DeQuan and Cedric sat in the middle of a game. He sat down and grabbed the score paper and pencil from Cedric.

"Everything good, bro?" asked DeQuan.

"Always. The fam said love, and they dropped $3 apiece on the books," James replied.

DeQuan and Cedric finished their game. James wanted in on the next game, so they played three way, taking out the cross blanks. They played until chow call. On their way out, Cedric noticed one of the Hispanic inmates watching him closely.

He nudged DeQuan in the side to get his attention. "What's up, youngster?" asked DeQuan.

"What's up with that Mexican over there? He been watching me all day," Cedric replied.

DeQuan didn't have to look around to know which one he was referring to. He'd peeped the move earlier. "Push up when we come from chow if you feel disrespected. You strolling with Slaughter Boyz, fam." He walked on out into the hallway.

They ate and walked back to the cellblock. When they entered the cellblock, Cedric didn't hesitate calling the Hispanic out. "Yo, homie, let me holla at you for a minute," he said, walking to the back of the cellblock.

The Hispanic inmate talked with the other Hispanics a moment longer, then walked over to see what he wanted. "What's up, homie?" he asked, standing out of striking distance.

"I was wondering the same thing, homie. You been had the beam down on me. What's up?" Cedric replied, adrenaline rushing through his body.

"Aye, homie, if you feel like I'm bitching you, let's shoot a fade," he said defensively.

"You speaking my language now," Cedric replied as he threw two quick jabs, catching the Hispanic off guard. He stumbled back and regained his footing. He blocked the next set of jabs Cedric threw at him.

James and DeQuan watched the fight from the domino table. They didn't know how good Cedric's fight game was, but they knew Chaves was a hard hitter. He use to fight pro. He was at the end of a bid for involuntary manslaughter, from beating his right hand man to death in public. High profile lawyers got him off easy because he was intoxicated when it happened.

Cedric and Chaves continued to stand toe to toe. Everybody who knew Chaves, knew he was only toying with Cedric because he really didn't want to fight. But, since Cedric wasn't understanding that, he went on and gave him what he'd asked for.

Cedric threw a left hook. Chaves weaved and caught him with two breathtaking body blows to the rib and kidney before taking him down with a left hook of his own to the jaw. Cedric was asleep on his feet. To avoid a possible charge, Chaves caught his unconscious body and eased him down to the concrete floor.

"Definitely not Slaughter Boy material," DeQuan stated and went back to washing the dominoes.

Chaves walked by the domino table and nodded to James and his brother. "Aye, big homies, the puta got balls, but he ain't got heart."

Neither said anything. DeQuan reached in his pocket, pulled out a balled-up piece of paper, and handed it to Chaves. "That's a Green Dot Money Pak Card for a $1. Good looking."

"Aye, anytime," Chaves replied and walked off to join his partners.

"Hopefully, the young nigga learned a lesson," James said.

"Bro, fuck dude. We used him for what he was worth." DeQuan replied and looked at the nine dominoes he'd pulled from the boneyard. "4 for 50."

Near the end of the game, Cedric finally regained consciousness. He picked himself up and wobbled over to the domino table and sat down. His pride was hurt, so he just sat quietly and watched the game. Knowing it, James and DeQuan had to stifle a laugh.

Willie Slaughter

Chapter Eight

Dink had called a South side Mafia Family meeting at the spot on Corn Street. It was Saturday, so Teddy and Mike were able to be in attendance. Everybody had shown dressed to impress. Teddy had insisted on the whole crew switching to a casual dress code instead of the typical dope boy attire. Nobody had complained or objected.

Dressed in Armani, Polo, and other brands of business suits, the crew sat in casual conversation, passing around blunts of different grades of marijuana while waiting on Dink to say whatever he had to say. After about the fourth rotation of blunts, he finally had his thoughts composed in a way to deliver it in words.

"What's good, family? Y'all bear with me and try to understand where a nigga coming from when I say this shit. Fam, something got to be done about this pig brutality. Young innocent niggas getting popped on the streets like they're target practice by one-time," Dink said. He paused for a minute and looked around the room. Everyone was following what he was saying, and some even looked mad.

"I know it ain't going down like that in Albany, but Albany is only one of the few cities pigs know better. To make a long story short, I'm going to put together a squad to even the playing field with these crooked-ass swine. I ain't asking for permission; I'm telling y'all, so there's no misunderstanding." Dink sat down.

Mike looked at Teddy, who sighed before standing up. "Bro, you know it's Slaughter Boyz and SMF for life. But, this save the world shit, is for dreamers. We got to worry about us. My nigga, we getting this paper, we eating, and nobody's starving or hurting for shit around us. You want to start your own security firm? That's some shit I'm down with. But all that Captain America shit ain't flying. Remember what we lost the last time your ass wanted to be selfish," Teddy reminded him.

The room was quiet. Dink was in deep thought. He understood where Teddy was coming from, and he knew everyone else did too. "You say start my own security firm, right?"

Teddy nodded. "Yeah. On some real live protecting the communities shit."

"Alright, fam, I'm with that. Just let me do my homework on the business and I'm going to hit you and Mike up one day next week," Dink replied. He was getting ready to leave when Henry told everybody to hold up for a second.

"We got 150 uncut bricks washing ashore midnight. Be on point for delivery. T will text everybody the pickup location after the shipment is transported to the secure spot," Henry said.

They left in an orderly fashion. Henry's report changed everybody's mood from fuck the police to grind mode.

***

Machumu found herself sitting at the beauty salon getting the full works: hair, manicure and facial. She was having a ball, indulging in the ladies' talk and listening to the music. It had been awhile since she treated herself to a woman's day out. But if Li'l Will was going to be all depressed, she was about to start treating herself more often.

Someone had entered the salon and caused everyone to stop talking. Machumu couldn't see who it was because of the cucumbers over her eyes, but when the woman spoke, her voice was undeniable.

"Hello, Machumu. Welcome to Valaire, one of my humble and humbling establishments," Renika said, using her professional tone of voice.

Machumu couldn't resist taking the cucumbers from over her eyes. It took a few seconds for her eyes to readjust to the brightly-lit salon. When they did, Renika, surrounded by three of her personal bodyguards, was standing directly in front of the station she was at.

"How are you feeling, Renika?" asked Machumu.

"Alicia, take ten," Renika demanded.

The young Asian woman walked off from the station without hesitation. Machumu noticed how fast she had obeyed her employer. "I see you have respect amongst your employees," Machumu said.

"Call it what you want to. My employees get paid whether they show up to work or not." Renika replied.

Her comment caused Machumu to take a good look around her for the first time since coming to Valaire. Every employee's body posture was the same as the bodyguards with her husband's daughter. "Dammit, man. I've been coming to a lion's den all along. Nice," Machumu stated.

"Yeah, it can use some improvements." Renika replied while surveying the salon. Everything was actually on point. There were twenty stations, all of which were one stop shops. You could get the hairstyle you wanted while getting a manicure and facial. Not to mention there was music, television, and a mini bar.

"Looks pretty laid to me," Machumu replied. She was a regular customer when she did treat herself.

"Thanks. Enjoy your day," Renika said and walked away, followed by her bodyguards.

Machumu placed the cucumbers back over her eyes as she saw Alicia returning to the station. She sighed, trying to relax. But it was kind of hard, knowing she was surrounded by undercover killers.

***

Li'l Will was sitting on the front porch smoking a blunt when his mother and the rest of the family came back from church. As always, Ruby was fired up. If nothing else got her to moving, a good church sermon always did the trick.

"Son, you missed a great sermon today. The reverend was filled with the Holy Spirit," his mother said. She looked at him, and could tell something was wrong. "Willie James, what's wrong with you?"

He took a deep drag and exhaled slowly. "Uncle James and DeQuan told me to tell you they love you. I sent them $300 apiece."

Dee, Li'l Bee, and his youngest daughter, Tara, tired from sitting for hours and eating so much food, walked on inside of the house, speaking as they passed by Li'l Will. His mother sat down beside him, holding her pocketbook in her lap.

"Well, that was very nice of you. Those jokers should be coming home in a few months."

Li'l Will nodded. "Yup. Seven months, to be exact," he reminded his mother before puffing on the blunt again.

"Who was it, that heathen wife or my granddaughter?" asked Ruby.

Li'l Will tried to hit the blunt again, but it had gone out. He sat the roach in the ashtray while saying, "A combination. By the way, Renika left today, and I don't think she is coming back again."

His mother could hear the hurt in his voice. She stood up. "Well, Willie James, count your many blessings. She's in good hands with the Lord. She's right to feel the way she feels." Ruby patted him on the shoulder. "Mama going to let you sit out here and figure out what you need to do. Whatever you deicide, just think about your family." She walked on into the house.

Once the front door closed, Li'l Will picked up the blunt roach out of the ashtray and fired it back up. His mind was really blank when it came to trying to reconcile with his oldest daughter. He knew it had to be done, but at the moment, it wasn't happening.

Willie Slaughter

Chapter Nine

Nicole was up early the next morning. She skipped breakfast and did not have the usual conversation with her husband before she decided how she was going to spend her day. She already knew. She grabbed the miniature size touchscreen cellphone out of her personal safe and the keys to the Range Rover and started towards the front door.

"Where you headed?" she heard Mark ask from behind her.

Nicole spun around on her heels wearing a serious facial expression. "Where does it look like I'm going?" she replied sarcastically.

By the looks of her, Mark could tell Nicole's outing was all business. She had on a forest green Ralph Lauren women's pantsuit with the six inch heels to match. "Have a safe business trip, luv," Mark said before kissing her on the lips.

She smiled. "I will. Just be ready to put me back in the mood your kiss just sparked when I get home," she replied before turning around and walking off.

As Nicole got behind the wheel of the Range Rover, the phone rang. She checked her personal phone first. Seeing it wasn't ringing, she immediately took out the miniature touchscreen cellphone. The screen was lit up with an incoming call that she answered after typing in the password.

"Hello?" Nicole said politely.

"Hi, my friend. It's Oman Jharez. I'm calling on the behalf of Valaire Perfecto," he replied in a serious tone of voice.

Nicole pulled out of the driveway. She waited until she was off of the premises to Bluetooth the phone where she could set it down and hear him through the speakers inside of the vehicle.

"Oh, hi Oman. I see you made it to safety. What do you have for me?" she said.

"Type in the code I'm about to send you via message. A road map will pop up on the screen, indicating the route to your destination," Oman replied.

The new text message icon popped up on the screen. Nicole pulled over on the side of the road. She opened the text message and memorized the three digit security code. She pulled up the number keys, typed in the code, and pressed enter.

A map with a line drawn through it appeared on the screen. There was a red blinking dot at one end of the line and a bullseye at the other. "Okay. I'm in," Nicole said.

"Good. I would like to thank you again, Nicole," Oman said with a hint of emotion sounding in his voice.

"If the shoe ever gets on the other foot, just return the favor," she replied while looking through the rearview mirror, making sure she wasn't being tailed.

"You're too smart of a woman, so I doubt if that'll ever happen. Besides, Valaire Perfecto Dominica wouldn't spare the bloodline of whoever tried to put on those shoes," he said, complimenting her.

"Understood. Let me get to the destination. I'll be in touch," Nicole said before ending the call.

The road map popped back up on the screen. As Nicole started driving, the blinking red dot began to move. She found a good instrumental disc to listen to while she drove. The music helped her prioritize her thoughts.

Nicole was going through what could possibly be the questions and answers conversation that awaited her when she looked through the rearview mirror and saw the black sedan on her tail. She could tell by the distance they stayed from her that whoever it was worked for her uncle. It made her smile. "Okay, Uncle Demetri, you just lost yourself a good tracker," she said out loud.

Nicole waited until she entered a zone where there wasn't any traffic before pulling in behind a mini market. She left the Range Rover gassing as she quickly jumped out and crept to the opposite side of the redbrick store. Just as she suspected, the sedan pulled in and slowly rode around to the rear of the store. She grabbed a blue and white LA Dodgers baseball cap off a sales table out front and put it on as a disguise.

Nicole crept up behind the sedan, which was a few feet from her vehicle, with her head down. She walked up to the driver's side and tapped on the window. The window slid down slowly, revealing the face of a Caucasian male, who looked to be in his early thirties.

"Yes, can I help you with something, ma'am?" asked the driver.

Nicole kept her head down so her face wouldn't be visible. She leaned on the door with her arms inside of the car. "Yes sir. I have a one way message to be delivered," she said before chopping the man in the throat.

He grabbed his neck, wheezing. Nicole got a glance at the pistol with a silencer on it inside the holster on his right side. She grabbed it and shot him twice in the head at point blank range.

"Teach you about sending someone to tail me," Nicole thought out loud as she hopped back in the Range Rover. She tossed the gun on the floorboard on the passenger side and drove off.

Back en route, she relaxed. Since her uncle had gone to the extreme of having someone watch her moves, Nicole knew something was wrong.

As she came to a complete stop at a red light, the phone rang. It was Valaire Perfecto.

"I'm on my way," Nicole answered.

"This I know, Nicole. I see you had made a pit stop. Is everything alright?" Dominica asked out of concern.

"Your husband sent one of his fucking cronies after me. I ain't mad because he sent him. I'm mad because he sent one damn person."

Dominica couldn't mistake the anger she was hearing in her niece's voice. "That's your Uncle Demetri. Always out to undermine those who he can't control or influence. I was just calling to make sure you didn't need any assistance. You're only an estimated thirty minutes out. I'll see you when you arrive," Dominica said and then hung up.

The light turned green, and Nicole mashed the gas. She was ready to hear what her aunty had to say.

***

Noon had come, and Mark was having a drink with Demetri, Thaddeus, and Damien. The four men sat at the mini bar enjoying each other's company. Damien, knowing his uncle, could tell Demetri was in deep thought because he was drinking clear instead of brandy. And he was knocking back shot after shot.

"Uncle Demetri, you feeling alright today?" asked Damien.

"That's a million dollar question," Demetri replied. He cut his eyes at Mark, saying, "Where the hell is your wife? Did she lose track of time?"

Mark hunched his shoulders. "She had some business to tend to. Don't ask me what or where because I have not a fucking clue."

"Mark, my man, you need to get that woman under control. She's a loose damn cannon. Ain't no way I would keep a hotheaded-ass woman like that around," Demetri said in a slurred voice.

Mark waved him off, not even trying to entertain his last statement. His gesture actually struck a nerve with Demetri.

"Boy, did you just brush me off?" asked Demetri as he stood up. "Answer me, dammit!"

Damien, not being much of a drinker, was still sober. He stood in between his uncle and brother-in-law. "Chill Unc. Mark, don't pay him any mind. He's had too much liquor."

Marked nodded and returned to the barstool. Demetri slapped his nephew's hand down. "You taking up for this nigger?" he said angrily.

There was complete silence in the room other than Thaddeus's glass slipping from his grip, shattering on the hardwood floor. "Demetri, what in the hell has gotten into you?" Thaddeus yelled.

"You should he asking Damien that, not me! I'm not going against family for a nigger!" Demetri held his left hand to his forehead, saying, "Oh, I forgot. Damien, you're half nigger yourself."

It took everything in Damien not to kill his uncle. "I'm going to pretend like I just didn't hear what you said. You're drunk and, for some reason, upset."

Demetri pushed passed him and stumbled over to the bar. "You ever heard the saying a drunk man never lies? Well, here is the truth. You and your half nigger sister and her nigger husband can stay the hell off my property."

Thaddeus had heard enough. He walked over to his twin brother, and punched him square in the jaw, causing him to flip over the barstool. "Demetri, how dare you insult family like this?" Thaddeus turned around to face his nephew and niece's husband. Shame was written all over his face. "Damien, Mark, I apologize for the behavior of my brother. He has truly brought shame upon us."

Mark, angry, but well-composed, nodded. "Thanks, Thad, but the shame belongs to Demetri alone. One thing he is right about: a drunk man always shows who the fuck they really is."

Damien grabbed Mark by the right shoulder. "Come on, bro. Let us niggers, as he called us, leave this miserable old man alone. Uncle Thaddeus, you know where to find us if you need us. But Demetri, fuck you," Damien said coldly before he and Mark left.

Thaddeus looked upon his brother with disgust. He didn't bother helping him up. Instead, he walked out of the room, leaving Demetri lying on the floor.

Chapter Ten

Nicole looked at the road map on the miniature screen. She was about three minutes out. She looked back up to see a row of Victorian style homes on her left, but there was an estimated fifteen foot high wall to her right, blocking the view to whatever was behind it. When she drove alongside the entrance gate, where two armed uniformed guards stood stationary, the phone made a chiming sound.

Nicole turned the music off and settled into her business frame of mind before steering the Range Rover up to the closed gate. She rolled down the window as one of the guards approached the vehicle. As the guard lifted her head, Nicole quickly noticed she was black. The awareness caught her by surprise.

"Name and identification?" asked the guard.

Nicole had purposely brought her maiden identification card. She passed it through the window to the guard. "Nicole Citural."

The guard had a smirk on her face while looking at the ID card. She handed it back to Nicole and said, "You were expected thirty minutes ago. Anyway, don't look so surprised when you get inside."

The guard stepped away from the vehicle while radioing for the gate to be opened. Nicole got a good look at her 5'9" frame, and could tell the woman was athletically built. The electronic gate slid open from the right. She drove on in.

Nicole had seen a lot of nice homes and had lived in quite a few herself, but not quite like this. "Dammit, man," she said in a low voice. Before her eyes was a compound. Not the usual styled compound, but a compound of mansions as far as her eyes could see.

The passenger side door opening and closing startled Nicole. "Don't need you getting lost. We all live peacefully here, but not all take too kindly to new faces, especially faces not as dark as theirs," The guard thrust her right hand out towards Nicole. "My name is Josephine Natalia Sylvan."

Nicole embraced her hand in hers. "I'm - "

"I already know who you are. Drive. Take a left at the next turn," Josephine said, cutting her off.

Nicole followed Josephine's directions as she continued to provide them. She pulled up before a solar power paneled three story mansion that she could tell was just as long as it was wide. Two guards, a man and woman dressed in deep forest green fatigues, stood at ease on each deck. Other than that, people of African descent seemed to be going about their day in a normal fashion.

A young man, who looked to be twenty years old, dressed in a valet's uniform, approached the vehicle. He opened the door for Nicole to get out. She grabbed her shoulder bag and got out. Remembering the pistol she'd thrown on the floorboard, she turned around just as the man was getting behind the wheel. "Hold on a second."

Standing on the other side of the Range Rover, Josephine held the gun up, causing her to stop in her tracks. "I'll hold on to this for you."

"Actually, you can get rid of it. It belonged to a dead man," Nicole replied.

Josephine nodded. "Hence the reason you were late. Come on, before your tardiness finds us both in trouble. Nobody bullshits around when summoned by Valaire Perfecto Dominica."

Nicole followed Josephine inside. Thinking the outside was nice, she was awed by the inside of the mansion.

Artifacts, portraits, and paintings of different sceneries in different countries lined the walls, all illuminated by candlelight.

The hardwood floor was a swirl of coffee brown, maroon, and burnt orange that complemented the same pattern on the hardwood walls. Nicole could tell the mansion held priceless history. She was so caught up in the art, she found herself bumping into Josephine, who had stopped before a set of double doors.

"Excuse me. This is one laid crib," Nicole said.

Josephine allowed a light smile to play upon her lips. "That it is. However, everything can be improved," she replied modestly and then opened the double doors. "Right this way."

They walked into the room, where a black woman, who looked to be in her mid-thirties, sat behind a large smoke grey marble top desk. Her long, silky black hair cascaded about her shoulders. From sitting position, she was about 5'10". The dark brown blouse she was wearing complemented her brown skin complexion.

"Your guest has arrived, Valaire Perfecto Dominica. Nicole Citural, meet Valaire Perfecto Dominica Citur," Josephine said by way of introduction and then left, closing the doors behind her.

Nicole remained standing until she was asked to be seated. "If I didn't know any better, I would say your curiosity brought you here. On the other hand, you weren't expecting to see what you see," Dominica said.

Nicole looked around the room. There were portraits of young and old people of African descent on the wall directly behind the desk. On the wall to her left were paintings of estates, lighthouses, seashores, and things of the nature. The wall to her right she found interesting because there were paintings of a younger version of Dominica and Demetri together.

Dominica followed her gaze and, with a straight face, said, "That was then, Nicole. A memory that I'm not too fond of. I'm sure you have your questions."

That she did. Nicole got comfortable in the high back leather padded chair. "Excuse my French, but I haven't seen one damn Turk since coming here. What's this bullshit about the Turks?" asked Nicole.

Dominica laughed. "Child, that's another illusion your uncle has fed you. My father employed the Turks to handle a certain portion of business that he wouldn't allow his own people handle because of the risks it ran."

Nicole nodded, understanding Dominica's father's methods. "A brilliant man. How did he end up losing to Demetri?"

"If you call poisoning a man's herbal tea a fair fight, then Demetri was victorious. But as you can see, Demetri's wealth is nowhere near the wealth of this compound alone," Dominica replied with confidence.

Dominica went on to tell her niece about the reason for her father's death. That Demetri was power struck, and wanted to control the drug business, something her father didn't really care about financing or indulging in. Her family members were legitimate business owners who owned diamond and gold mines in certain countries of Africa and Asia, not to mention the investments into the oil industry in Alaska and offshore rigs.

Nicole listened like a student in social studies class. Dominica started from the time of her and Demetri meeting and ventured through history. When she spoke of the day of her father's death, her voice became full of emotion.

"Yeah, I remember that day like it was just yesterday. Once we found out Demetri had ordered the hit on my father, we packed up and left the estate, knowing his greed would lead to him ordering the death of the rest of us. We moved back here, to the main compound, where we knew no one had the guts to come starting trouble." Dominica paused, reliving the memory.

Nicole was bound between hate and murder. She'd known her Uncle Demetri to be a cruel man, but not to the extent she was learning. "So, if he sent someone to try to kill me, what about - Shit!" Her mind went to her husband Mark. She jumped up out of the chair to leave.

"Sit down, Nicole. You're probably already too late," Dominica said.

***

Damien had walked Mark home and left. Tipsy and angry, Mark went straight upstairs and jumped in the shower. For the first time in a long time, he'd witnessed racism. Personally, he'd never disrespected another ethnic group of people, and he definitely didn't appreciate it when someone disrespected his or anybody else's.

He made a mental note to call Li'l Will and tell him about the situation. He also would say something to his wife when she got home. Mark punched the tile wall of the shower. He couldn't get the scene off repeat within his mind.

The way Demetri used the term "nigger" gave Mark a new profound disrespect for him. Thaddeus, on the other hand, proved to be of a different breed. The thought of Thaddeus standing up for him and Damien calmed his nerves. He turned off the water and got out of the shower.

Mark wrapped the drying towel about himself before walking out of the bathroom just in case one of Nicole's female family members had come looking for him. The drapes were drawn shut and the lights were off, so the bedroom was in darkness, which was the reason he didn't notice the man standing in the fold of the drapes. Mark sat on the edge of the bed, enjoying the peace within the quietness.

The man, dressed in dark clothing, screwed the silencer on the .45 caliber handgun. Instead of showing his hand, he squeezed the trigger twice, hitting Mark in the back with both shots. Mark rolled off the edge of the bed onto the carpeted floor wheezing because one of the bullets had punctured a lung. As he made an attempt to crawl to where his gun was, the man came from behind the drapes and put two more bullets in the back of his head and left Mark for dead.

***

Damien wanted to call his sister to check up on her because it wasn't like her to be gone for long periods of time and not check in, letting him know where she was. He reached for his iPhone, but the case was empty. He realized he'd left it on the coffee table in the den at Nicole and Mark's estate. Although halfway home, he turned around, heading back to get his phone.

Damien pulled halfway up the driveway and stopped. There was a lot of commotion going on out front and the paramedics were carrying someone out on the stretcher. Whoever it was, by their body being covered, it was clear they were dead.

Damien put the 500 Mercedes Benz in park and hopped out at a sprint. He reached the paramedics before they put the body in the back of the ambulance. "Hold on a second!" he yelled at the EMT.

They stopped, holding the stretcher. Damien peered beneath the white sheet and cringed upon seeing Mark's lifeless corpse. "Son of a bitch!" was all he could muster up the strength to say.

Damien ran on into the house, where his mother sat in tears. It was obvious nobody knew what had happened, so he didn't bother asking. He checked on everybody else to make sure nobody else was injured or dead. Afterwards, he grabbed his iPhone off the coffee table in the den and left.

Back in his car and driving, Damien called his sister on speed dial. She didn't answer the first time. He got the voicemail. "Pick up your damn phone!" he yelled and then hung up. He called again, and this time she answered on the third ring.

"If you're calling to inform me that my husband is dead, save it, because I already know," Nicole said, coldly answering her phone.

Damien was confused. "How in the fuck do you already know? What in the hell is going on?" he demanded to know.

Nicole sighed. "Motherfuckers ain't who you think they are, Damien. Demetri sent a hitter at me earlier."

"What? Are you okay?" Damien said, cutting his sister off.

"I'm great, bro," she replied. "But listen."

Nicole filled him in on everything she'd learned. After all he'd experienced today, nothing she was saying was farfetched. He told her about their confrontation and how Thaddeus attacked Demetri for bringing them shame. That got a laugh out of her, but he could tell Nicole was upset about Mark's death. The pain was unmistakable in her voice.

"So, all of this shit about him being The Head was a hoax?" asked Damien.

"Damien, I'm sure the true Valaire Perfecto would love to meet her nephew," Nicole replied.

"Oh yeah? What makes you think that, sis?" he asked.

"Because I'm sitting here with her," she said, sounding a little annoyed. She cut him off before he could respond, saying, "I'm sending a link via Gmail to your phone. Do you have it?"

Damien looked at the screen. The Gmail popped up in the left hand corner. He opened up his Gmail. "Yeah, sis, I got it. Now what?"

"Open the link. Type in 333. That's the pass code."

Damien did exactly what his sister told him. A map with a line drawn through it appeared on the screen. There was a red blinking dot at one end of the line and a bull's-eye at the other. "I'm in. I'll see you when I get there." He hung up.

Chapter Eleven

Nicole hung up the phone and set it on the marble desk. Knowing what was about to happen, Dominica stood up for the first time since she'd gotten there. She walked around the desk and took a seat in the chair beside Nicole before placing a gentle hand on her shoulder, saying, "The show of emotions only makes you look weak when you can't control the action or reaction it surfaces, Nicole."

"The bastard killed my husband," Nicole cried. The tears were pouring.

Dominica took her niece into her arms and held her close. "Don't worry, baby. We're going to get his good for nothing ass. And when we do, his bitch ass is going to suffer. I promise you."

***

Demetri took a cold shower to sober up. Where he hadn't felt the pain in his jaw before, the pain had become visible and the ache was real. Looking in the mirror, he rubbed his jaw and winced at the soreness. "That was a hell of a punch," he thought out loud.

The memory of the confrontation between him and his nephew and Mark was still fresh in his mind. Thinking about all that he'd set in motion prior to their heated war of words, Demetri smiled. It was a devious smile. "I will always win," he said to himself, still staring at himself in the mirror.

A knock came at the bathroom door. Demetri put on a robe, covering himself before telling them to come in. It was his brother Thaddeus. And by the look on his face, Demetri knew a portion of his plan had gone as planned.

"We have a situation on our hands. Mark was found dead with four bullet wounds inside of his own home," Thaddeus informed him.

Inside, Demetri was smiling. His brother's facial expression was priceless. "Probably those damn sneaky Turks. We need to retaliate, hit them hard and fast," Demetri replied.

That, Thaddeus wasn't buying. "Demetri, I said he was found inside of his own goddam house dead. To be precise, inside of his bedroom. How the fuck would a Turk make it in the house and all the way up the stairs to the bedroom without being spotted by security? Who the fuck do you take me for, Demetri?"

Demetri chuckled. "Well, Thaddeus, the nigger had it coming to him. How about that for an answer?"

Thaddeus frowned, but then it dawned on him. "You sick son of a bitch!" he exclaimed and stepped towards his brother.

Demetri stepped back and braced himself against the bathroom sink. "Business is business, bro. I can't have what we've built be destroyed by a nigger and a half breed. No matter if the half breed is my niece."

Thaddeus shook his head in disgust. "You know what? Fuck you, Demetri." He stormed out of the bathroom.

Demetri's cell phone vibrated on the countertop. "What information do you have for me?" he answered, skipping formalities.

"Your man was made. Target terminated him," the caller replied.

Demetri sighed out of frustration. "Alright." He hung up. He knew it would be useless and a suicide mission to tell him to pursue Nicole. He set the phone back on the counter and sat on the toilet in deep thought. He knew Nicole had to be silenced before she could cause disaster.

***

Due to his shitty attitude lately, Li'l Will had decided to take Machumu out. It was one way of him apologizing and to avoid thinking about decisions he had to make. He took her to a nice live jazz spot in the downtown area. It was a nice setup, a canopy-covered outside dining area that his wife immediately fell in love with.

"Mr. James, how long have you known about this spot? You know how much I love places like this. It reminds me of back home," Machumu said.

Her family was originally from the islands. They had moved to the States to try to avoid the political drama that never ceased.

"I'm glad you like it, baby. It's the least I can do to show you I'm sorry for my fucked-up attitude," Li'l Will replied before waving over a waitress.

They ordered a seafood platter for two, a red velvet cake, and a bottle of Dom. The waitress took their order and left. Li'l Will turned to his wife and held her hands in his before saying, "So, tell me about your experience before coming to the States?"

The question caught her by surprise. All the years they had been together, it was the first time he ever asked about her life on the islands. "I grew up in a political household. My father was Chief of Security Staff and my mother was Assistant Secretary of State."

Li'l Will cut her off, saying, "Now I know why your ass is so damn bossy."

Her eyes widened. "I'm not bossy! I just know how to keep that ass in check."

He chuckled. "I can't argue with you there. Back to you though."

"Oh yeah." Machumu continued, "So, election time on the islands is like watching the Watts riots on repeat every fucking day until it is over. People rioting, killing government officials, police, and each other over a mother fucker who could give less than one red cent about them. My mother and father started seeing how the bullshit was coming too close to home when my Uncle Musa got necklaced in front of his wife and kids in broad daylight."

"Necklaced?" asked Li'l Will not quite knowing what she meant.

Machumu explained it to her husband: being beaten and having a rubber tire put around the body with gasoline inside of the rim of the tire as well as the body being drenched in gasoline, and being set on fire. "So, if you ever experience seeing someone getting necklaced up close in person, you will never forget the shit. Trust me."

Li'l Will shook his head. "I think I'll pass," he replied, staring into her eyes. "Continue, luv."

Machumu went on and on about the political scheme that led to her and her family moving to the States, how the majority of her family settled in Italy, where they had their own compound. It was during one of their visits to the compound that she met Demetri and Thaddeus, who worked for her grandfather at the time.

"Hold on a minute." Li'l Will said, interrupting her. "Demetri and his brother used to work for your grandfather?"

Machumu nodded. "Yup. I see you find it surprising."

He was about to respond when the waitresses brought their order and set it on the table. He thanked them by giving each of the three waitresses a ten dollar tip. Machumu smiled at how pleasant he was being. "Aren't you being the gentle and kind giant today? I got to think of a great way to reward you, Mr. James," she said in a soft, seductive manner. "You don't have to think too hard, luv," he replied.

They ate the seafood platter and red velvet cake and drank their champagne while allowing the rhythm of the live jazz take their minds to comfortable memories. They finished their meal and champagne.

Machumu reared back in the chair, rubbing her stomach. "Dammit, I'm stuffed. I got to work this off."

Li'l Will called a waitress over and asked for the bill. She walked off, saying she would be right back. In her absence, he told his wife he wanted to hear more about her family, but not today. "All I'm interested in hearing is your sexy ass moaning in my ear for the rest of the day," he said right before the waitress returned with the bill.

Li'l Will paid the tab and left a twenty dollar bill tip on the table for whoever cleaned it. He and his wife made their way to their metallic black 750 BMW. "Where are we going now?" asked Machumu, reclining in the passenger seat.

"I made arrangements at the Marriott for us. It's been awhile since we had a day to ourselves," Li'l Will replied.

So far, so good, he thought to himself as he drove into the flow of traffic. Sundays were always good traveling days in his eyes because of the lack of heavy traffic. They made it to the Marriott in no time. Li'l Will checked them in at the front desk, and they walked hand in hand to the suite.

Machumu hung the do not disturb sign on the outside doorknob and locked the door after they entered the room. "I'm going to make this a day you are going to remember," Machumu said, taking off her clothes.

Li'l Will was undressed within seconds. They lay in the king size waterbed facing each other, kissing. Machumu rolled over on top of him and kissed him on the lips passionately before turning around on top and grabbing hold of his sex. She stroked him slowly and wrapped her lips around him and began sucking him off.

"Dammit, girl," Li'l Will said, loving the way her thick lips felt gliding up and down the length of his dick. "Do your thang." He palmed her booty with both hands and dove face first in between her cheeks, licking up and down the length of her opening and clitoris.

"Yes, big daddy, it's an all you can eat buffet," she said softly in between moans.

They 69'ed it out. Li'l Will and Machumu moaned and groaned to the pleasure they were giving each other. It was hard to tell who was the loudest. His toes were curled and her body was trembling.

"Oh Willie!" she cried, throwing her booty back onto his face. "Damn, your tongue feels so good! That's it! Tongue this pussy down, baby! Mmm." Machumu bobbed up and down his shaft faster and faster.

"Oooh shit! I'm 'bout to cum, baby!" Li'l Will yelled.

Machumu sat up straight on her knees before maneuvering her body down. She rose up and slowly eased down on top of him facing backwards. She rode him like a bucking bronco.

"That's what I'm talking 'bout, girl! Ride this dick!" Li'l Will yelled. He slapped her playfully on her booty, causing her to moan louder and her pussy to become wetter.

Feeling herself about to cum, Machumu held on to his legs and started popping on top of him hard and fast until she came. She grinded her release on out. "Oh, baby," she moaned.

Before he could say anything, she slid up to where only the head of his sex was penetrating her and started popping real fast on the tip. Li'l Will's mind was running wild. He didn't know whether to grab her thighs or the sheets.

"Damn, I love you so much, Machumu! I'm…I'm… Oh shit!" He came hard inside of her.

Once she felt his release flowing, Machumu came down hard on top of him and rocked back and forth. His legs shook and her body shook even harder. Just looking at her plush, round booty from behind aroused him again. She felt him harden inside of her and laid back on top of him.

Li'l Will short stroked inside of her hard and fast. She moaned and called out his name, enjoying the erotic moment. They came together. Machumu rolled off top of him onto the bed and faced him.

"Now, that's what I call getting sexed, baby," she said in a sexy voice before kissing him on the lips.

Li'l Will kissed her back. "Hell yeah. We have this whole day to be on our worst behavior."

They took a nap, holding each other. But when one or both of them woke up, it was back to getting their freak on.

***

Renika was chilling at her studio apartment, one of the many spots she had. Cedric hadn't called her since the night she chomped him off and hung up in his face. That didn't bother her though. Not as much as the episode with her father.

She was snacking on a bag of trail mix when her iPhone started ringing. The ringtone playing was Scarface's "Scratch", so she knew who was calling.

"What's up, Nicole? How you living?" asked Renika.

Nicole sighed. "If only you knew. But that's why I'm calling you, to fill you in."

Renika sat up straight and put down the bag of trail mix. Nicole had her interest. "You got my attention. What's going on? Do I need to take a trip?"

"We'll cross that bridge if or when it becomes necessary. Brace yourself for the shit I'm about to put on you," Nicole replied.

"Come on with it," Renika said.

Nicole gave Renika the rundown on what had happened and what was going on. Renika was astounded. She put the phone on speakerphone, set it on the coffee table, and picked up the bag of trail mix. She snacked and listened to the most interesting news she'd heard in a long time.

"Old slick-ass Demetri," Renika commented. "Oh shit!" she exclaimed, remembering it was Demetri who put her father on top. "This means the whole thing about my pops being the new head is some bullshit."

"Well, as far as the dope game goes, he is the head. But if you want to talk about what's really going on, hell no, Li'l Will ain't running shit. Neither is Demetri or Thaddeus. All of it is a web built by some straight sucker shit," Nicole replied.

"Let me delete his racist pale ass out of my contacts." Renika said and picked up her iPhone. She deleted Demetri's number from her contacts and blocked him from calling. "As much as I would like to see my pop's ass suffer, I got to hit him up and give him the 4-1-1."

Nicole laughed. "Understood. Just hit me back a little later." She hung up.

Renika scrolled through her contacts, looking for Li'l Will's number. She found it and called him. The phone rang until the voicemail came on. She immediately hung up.

"I'm not talking to a damn automated voice." She thought out loud. She called back again, and this time, got an answer.

"Hello?" Machumu said, sounding worn out.

Renika couldn't suppress the laughter. "Sounds like somebody's been through it. It's Renika, Machumu. Put your husband on the phone."

Machumu tapped Li'l Will on the shoulder while calling his name. He woke up, saying, "I can't go another round, baby. You win."

"No, baby. Your daughter is on the phone. She needs to talk to you." Machumu replied while yawning.

"Which daughter?" asked Li'l Will as he rolled over to face her.

"Just take the damn phone, man," she demanded.

Li'l Will grabbed the phone out of Machumu's hand. She rolled over and went back to sleep.

"Hello?" he answered, yawning.

"Damn, is everybody wore out? You going for baby number four or five, Pops?" Renika said teasingly.

He chuckled. "Renika, how are you doing? Is everything okay?"

"Actually, yes and no. I would beat your ears up with the truth of the matter, but I've decided to send it to you via text message. Call me back once you're done reading it," Renika said.

"Okay, I will," Li'l Will replied.

"Oh, I know you will, Pops." She hung up.

Before she could set the phone back down, a text message came through on her private sector. She opened it and smiled. It was a contract from an employer who wanted it filled ASAP. The text message read, "Blood for Blood," with a $250K deposit notice attached.

Renika texted back immediately. All she wanted to know was who the target was and the location. The employer sent another text message that had an image attached to it, waiting to be downloaded. The text message read, "Target on the move. Will have actual location for you momentarily. Don't care how target is terminated. Only ask kill confirmed."

It was Renika's favorite kind of contract. She pressed download, and waited for the attachment to upload in the image viewer. When the picture and name of the target popped up on the screen, she laughed and texted back, stating, "Waiting for location verification."

"Sit tight. You will have all info soon," the employer replied in a text.

With her phone in hand, Renika walked to the refrigerator, opened it, and grabbed a bottle of Gatorade. She shut the door of the refrigerator and returned to the couch. Before she could unscrew the cap on the bottle, she had an incoming call. It was from her father.

"Daddy, I don't have time for a thousand questions right now, so if you can't sum up what you got to say in less than ten minutes, it's going to have to wait," Renika answered, getting to straight to the point.

"Understood. I just wanted to tell you, that's some hard-core shit you just laid on me. I've been played like a fucking fiddle all along," Li'l Will said, voice full of anger.

"Everybody plays the fool sometimes," Renika replied before asking, "Is that all you have to say? Because I got money on my mental at the moment. No disrespect."

"Machumu wants to holler at you." He handed the phone to his wife.

"Renika, what's going on?" asked Machumu.

"Money. What's up? Y'all on money time," Renika reminded her.

"I just want to fill you in on the rest of the tea. Charles and Havenna Sylvan are my grandparents on my mother's side of my family. Dominica is my mother's oldest sister," Machumu replied.

The look on Renika's face was priceless. She took a swig of the Gatorade before responding. "Dammit man! You're the niece of Valaire Perfecto Dominica?"

Machumu chuckled. "From the womb to the tomb. Do you know what Valaire Perfecto means? It is a mixture between Swahili, French, Italian, and Patois and a more ancient language not too many people speak now days, meaning, The Perfect Black Source."

Renika took another swig, nodding to herself while processing what Machumu said. "That explains everything."

"How so?" asked Machumu.

"It was fucking impossible for Demetri or his brother to be Valaire Perfecto, so he came up with this I'm The Head bullshit. And due to the fact that my father is black, he played him to the left by putting him in a phony-ass position," Renika stated.

Machumu could hear the anger in her voice. "Yeah, that pretty much sums shit up. I guess my question is, what are we going to do about the situation?"

Renika looked at the screen of her iPhone X. The private sector text message icon flashed across the screen.

"Hello? Renika?" Machumu said.

"Just chill. I'm working on that now." Renika opened up her private message inbox. The information she needed to fill the contract had come through. "Alright, this phone call just expired. I'll call you back once I'm done working," she promised before hanging up.

Renika texted the employer back, letting them know she'd received the confirmed location and she was preparing to fulfil the contract. After she sent the text, Renika texted two of her personal crew members, telling them to meet her at the airport with their toys in about fifteen minutes. Both replied with the thumbs up emoji. She smiled, thinking to herself, *What a hell of a world.*

Chapter Twelve

Dink was setting everything in motion. He had called a meeting with his personal hitters and gave them the ups on what he envisioned to be a revolution. Trey, who was 6'5" and, 246 pounds of muscle, dark brown skin, and wavy hair, was his number one hitter. It didn't matter: hands on, gunplay or knife play, he was with it.

Trey's family was originally from Oakland, California, so Dink already knew he was with the revolution. He had a black panther tatted on his right forearm. "Homie, you know I'm ten toes down 'til the casket drops when it comes to the revolution," Trey said.

Dolo stated he was down with whatever. He was 5'7", 165 pounds, with light brown skin, hazel brown eyes, and he wore his hair in a ponytail. He was Albany born and raised. He Dink grew up together, staying into more shit than their parents knew.

Dolo's thing was gunplay. Put any kind of gun in his hand, and you got yourself a real live black Billy the Kid, Doc Holiday, or Wyatt Earp. Their home girl Kaila was the same. She was, boot black 5'3", 128 pounds, with long natural braided hair, a walking terrorist.

Kaila had a reputation for busting her guns and playing the box cutter game. She nodded while hitting the blunt, letting them know she was in on the movement. Her girlfriend China, who was 4'10" and 119 pounds, was black mixed with Chinese. She was so sexy that men and women alike always gave Kaila props on bagging her.

China was a natural bad ass. Her hands and feet were official and registered. She told Dink she was down, but only because her bae, Dae-Dae, Tiptoe, Block, and Santana were down as well.

"Alright, peep game," Dink said before hitting the blunt. "My brother said he is going to help a nigga start a security firm, but fuck all that. We going to do this shit Black Panther Georgia style. Matter of fact, that's our name, GA Black Panthers."

"Fucking right, homie!" Trey yelled.

Everybody was feeling the name. Dink knew, no matter what, his hitters were always with whatever movement he was putting down. Mostly because they were so much alike: grimy as hell.

"From now on, every time we hear about a cop killing one of our people or a pig on their brutality shit, we taking off on one of theirs. We ain't doing shit to get caught up. We moving in silence." Dink said.

Nobody disagreed with him. They sat, kicking it, smoking and drinking until everybody decided to leave.

***

Tanji and her mother were on the job. They'd received a call from the Bureau about a multiple homicide, which wasn't unusual in Boston, Massachusetts. Gang violence was almost like turning on the television, watching *Wildin' Out*. The shit was real, especially on the side of town the murders had happened on.

Director Harris walked around the bodies of the young black teens. Three of them were boys and the other two were girls. None were older than seventeen years old. Looking at the gunshot wounds, she shook her head, angry. She was more angry at the system than those who had done the killing.

"You might want to see this, Director Harris." Agent Harris ran over to where the director stood speechless.

She followed her daughter, Agent Harris, into the house. Bullet holes were scattered along the walls. They entered a bedroom that looked to be undisturbed by the investigators who were searching the house, gathering evidence.

"I'm the only one who's been in this room. Lucky me." Agent Harris flipped the top mattress over, revealing a mattress stuffed with money, drugs and guns."

"Damn," the director said, surprised.

"That was my expression too," Agent Harris replied. She looked around to make sure no one was within earshot of their conversation. "So, Director Harris, how are we playing this?"

Director Harris looked around the room. When she didn't find anything resembling what she was looking for, she had another bright idea. "Wait right here. I'll be back in a second." She trotted out of the bedroom.

The director returned carrying a body bag. "Okay, we got to do this quick. We're taking the money, but leaving the dope and guns for the investigators." She started tossing the money that was in bundles separated by rubber bands into the body bag. Agent Harris gave her hand with it.

After they had stuffed the body bag, Sarah ran out of the room again. This time she returned pushing a stretcher. "Let's get this body on the stretcher and out of this room, Agent Harris."

Agent Harris grabbed one end and Director Harris grabbed the other. "One, two, three. Lift!" Director Harris said. They lifted the black body bag onto the stretcher. Agent Harris strapped it down like a real body.

As they were rolling the body out, the investigators were coming in. The director, being quick with her thinking, told them about the stash of drugs and guns inside of the mattress, knowing it would take their focus off of the body on the stretcher. And it worked like a charm for her and Agent Harris.

"Bring the car alongside the ambulance and pop the trunk," she told her daughter, who didn't hesitate to follow orders.

Agent Harris hurried over to the unmarked black sedan and jumped behind the wheel. She drove around to the blind side of the ambulance. She opened the glove compartment and pressed the button to open the trunk before hopping out to help her mother with the body bag. They tossed the bag into the trunk and the agent eased the trunk closed.

"Nice work, Director Harris," Agent Harris said just in case someone was wandering around the area. She jumped back in the sedan and drove back around to where everyone could see the car, and waited on her mother to give her final set of orders.

Calling her subordinates to her, Director Harris barked out the instructions. She wanted the scene to remain taped off and the house too just in case there was a need for a more thorough search of the premises. "Good job, people! I'll see you guys at the office at 1600 hours!" She got in on the passenger side of the unmarked black sedan.

Agent Harris drove off, heading in the direction of headquarters. But once they were disguised in a steady flow of traffic, she got off on the nearest exit and headed for the director's home on the lake. "Great job for real, Director Harris," Tanji commended her mother with a sense of humor.

"Your finding, Agent Harris," Sarah replied.

"Our keeping," Tanji stated.

They rode in silence, listening to the police scanner the rest of the way. They made it to their destination. Sarah and her daughter grabbed the body bag out of the trunk and carried it inside into the den, where they sat down and counted it. "$378,000 isn't a bad lick," Tanji said after they were done counting.

"Definitely not when it's tax free money," her mother replied.

The two women laughed. "What time is it?" asked Tanji, looking at her Citizen Echo watch. It was 2:57 p.m.

"Why? What's up?" her mother asked.

Tanji took out her GalaxyS10. "I was supposed to call Damien and give him my yea or nay today," she replied as she called him. The phone rung twice before he answered.

"Hey. What's good, Tanji?" Damien said.

"That's the first time your phone ever rang twice when I called you," she replied.

"Seriously, Tanji, I'm in traffic and some real heavy shit is going down. I mean, you wouldn't believe it. Anyway, what's on my baby's mind?" he said.

"Yes," she responded.

"Yes? Yes what?" asked Damien, keeping his eyes on the GPS road map.

"Yes, I'm marrying you, crazy-ass man. So handle your business and call me back when you're available," Tanji demanded.

"I'm always available for you, Tanji. On the real, y'all might want to lay low for a while. This shit is about to hit the fan, and I don't want you or my mother-in-law caught up in it," Damien replied. He looked at the GPS, and it was reading he was only ten minutes away from his destination. "Listen, babes, I got to go. You and your mother can go ahead and turn in your resignation papers." He hung up.

Tanji hung up and looked at her mother, who was waiting on the news. "Mama, excuse my language, but it's some serious shit going on in Italy," she said. She filled her mother in on the information Damien had given her.

Sarah nodded her head in deep thought as she listened to her daughter. "Shit!" she exclaimed. "Looks like early retirement is what's happening," she said.

"Yeah, we was on point with that idea," her daughter replied.

Sarah jumped up off the couch. "Pack your bags," she said.

Tanji looked at her mother confused. "For what? What's up?" she asked.

"We're going to Italy," Sarah answered while walking out of the den to go pack.

***

Cedric and Tiffany had been going strong. She had even started bringing him cans of Buglers, ounces of marijuana, and lighters to hustle. It was definitely a help since he had not called Renika after the night she chomped him off and hung up in his face. He hadn't reached out to her for anything, nor did she volunteer to send him anything either.

He was really in grind mode. To him, it was like he wasn't really locked up. He kicked it with Tiffany on the phone every day when she got off work and on her off days. When she was at work, they always managed to do their thing in the control booth.

"I'm going to surprise her ass today," Cedric thought out loud as he ordered Tiffany a gift basket from an online delivery company and paid for it via Green Dot. Everything he hustled, he split 50/50 with her on Cash App. They were living the chain gang fame. After he completed the order, Cedric turned his phone off and put it up before leaving his cell. He sat down next to James at the domino table. Not really wanting to play, but he was waiting on Tiffany to walk her fine ass down the hallway. It was his daily routine.

"What's good, big homies? Let me get in next game," Cedric said.

DeQuan looked at him out of the corner of his eyes. "Li'l nigga, don't come with that elementary-ass playing, fucking up my winning streak," he said warningly.

Cedric checked the time on his watch. It was 1:45 p.m. He looked out of the large window, knowing his girl would be coming down the hallway any minute. "Big homie, you know my game is official," he replied.

James had peeped the move, and called him out on it. "Fam, this nigga sprung on the pussy. He ain't really out here to slam bones for real. He waiting on ole girl to bring her ass in."

The two brothers laughed. DeQuan shook his head. "Hell nah, young blood, your ass ain't playing," DeQuan said while laying the cross sixes.

Cedric didn't know how to respond. He had been called out, and James was right. Not to mention, his face lit up when he looked up and saw her walking down the hall. Unlike usual, he realized Tiffany wasn't smiling, but had a serious look in her eyes when she looked at him.

She must be PMS'ing, he thought to himself as he watched her enter the booth. He sat for a few more minutes after the other guard left. Concerned, Cedric hurried into his cell, put a blanket at the bottom of the door to muffle the sound, and pressed the intercom button. He heard it buzz on.

"Tiffany, is everything good?" he asked.

She was quiet for a moment. Actually, she was trying to put it in the best way. "I'm good, bae. I got that package for you. We'll talk later on," Tiffany replied.

Cedric sighed, relieved to know she hadn't been caught up bringing in the pack for him. "Okay, luv. I thought maybe it was that time of the month for you," he said.

She laughed nervously. "No. I doubt if I'll be seeing that for a while. Listen, bae, let me get situated. Besides, y'all about to go to chow," she replied.

Cedric could hear the kitchen guard calling over the radio, telling Tiffany to put their dorm on standby for chow. "Alright, luv, I'll talk to you later," he said and laid down. He decided to take a nap instead of going to chow. He was straight in the box and he knew, messing with Tiffany, he was going to need some energy.

Cedric was awakened from his sleep by a knock at the cell door.

"Mail call!" James yelled.

Cedric got up and grabbed his toothbrush and toothpaste. He walked out of the cell brushing his teeth. He went to the booth to get his mail. The way Tiffany was looking at him, his first thought was that it had to be a letter from Renika.

As Tiffany handed him the mail, he grabbed her hand and gently squeezed, causing her to smile. "Whatever is going on, we going to be alright, luv. I promise." Cedric said reassuringly. He looked at the envelope. The letter was from his lawyer.

"Yeah, I know, bae. Your ass is full of surprises," she said, referring to the gift basket she had received.

Cedric opened the letter in front of her and read it. "Oh shit! My appeal was granted!" He looked up at Tiffany. "My appeal was granted!" he said happily.

"Inmate Livingston, please return to your cellblock! There are other people who need to get their mail!" she said over the intercom.

He understood she had to play the part because of the circumstance. He strolled back into the dorm as happy as ever. Time flew by. The next thing he knew, he and Tiffany were making love in the booth on an extra mat he'd dragged into the booth from the hallway.

It was more time consuming than it had ever been between them. They explored each other's body with tender care. They moaned between kisses. After forty-five minutes of slow grinding together, they climaxed together and lay holding each other.

"I love you, Cedric," she said.

"I love you too, Tiffany," he replied.

"Cedric, I'm pregnant," Tiffany blurted out.

Cedric sat straight up. "Are you serious?" he yelled.

She put her left hand over his mouth. "Sh... Stop damn screaming, boy. Remember where you're at." she reminded him. "Yes, I'm serious. Are you upset?"

Cedric kissed her on the lips. "Why would I be upset? We're about to be a family. Married and everything," he replied.

"Thanks, bae. Thanks for not being a deadbeat-ass nigga." Tiffany commented.

They made love again before Cedric grabbed the package she'd brought and headed back in the cellblock. He knew he had to grind harder now that Tiffany was pregnant, he thought to himself as he jumped in the shower. "What a hell of a life," he said under his breath, thinking about his future.

Chapter Thirteen

Dink and his hitters were on the move. He'd just received an NBC News update on his iPhone, reading, "cop shoots unarmed black teen in the back". The sixteen-year-old male died at the scene from multiple gunshot wounds to the back. It was all he needed to hear.

"Listen, fam, we collecting a badge for every slug the swine put into the li'l nigga's back," Dink said as he loaded the AK-47. He had gotten them specially-made shell catchers so there would be no evidence left on the scene.

Trey hit the blunt and passed it to Kaila, who was loading a Mac-11, using a green bandana to put each bullet in the magazine. "Fucking right, homie, we going to make sure the li'l homie rest in peace," Trey said.

China was the driver. She rolled up on the first on duty cop in a suburban residential area. The patrol car was parked at the end of the street. The officer, himself, was talking to his wife on the phone.

After they rode around the block once, peeping the scenery, Dink put the blunt out. "Y'all know I ain't never been the nigga to tell someone to do some shit I ain't willing to do. I got this pig," he said.

The young Caucasian officer was in a great mood. His wife had just told him she was pregnant, so they were making plans for their child when Dink jumped out of the side sliding door of the bowling ball blue Dodge Caravan and shot him four times in the chest with the AK-47. He snatched the officer's badge off of his shirt and jumped back in the van. China pulled off before the door slid closed.

The officer's wife had heard the gunshots loud and clear. She kept calling her husband's name and asking if he was alright, but he never responded. He was dead.

"Next badge on me, my nigga," Trey said, hyped up.

Dink and his crew kept to their word. Four cops died on behalf of the number of times the cop shot the teenage boy. It didn't take long for the cop killings to go viral. And it took even lesser time for Teddy to call Dink.

"Fam, I thought we had an understanding. No vigilante shit," Teddy said angrily after Dink answered.

"Bro, I hear what you saying, but that shit ain't what's popping. We got to show these mother fuckers we ain't having it in Albany," Dink shot back.

Teddy sighed out of frustration. "Fam, the shit y'all got going on is bad for business. Y'all niggas going to have the Feds breathing down a nigga back," he said.

"They can get it too, li'l bro. Them pigs ain't exempt from catching a slug," Dink replied.

"See, that's your fucking problem, Dink. You don't give a damn about what nobody got going on. The world don't revolve around you, my nigga," Teddy said harshly.

Dink laughed. "Damn, fam, you sound like that nigga Li'l Will. Well, guess what, my nigga? Fuck you too." he stated and hung up in his brother's face. He tried to call him back, and every time Dink sent his call to voicemail.

***

Renika and her crew were at the airport. Amara, a Vietnamese was an explosive specialist. She was twenty-three years old, 4'11", 116 pounds, deeply tanned with long dyed burgundy hair that reached halfway down her back. Danika, a Russian, was the technician of the crew. She was thirty-one years old, 6'2", 167 pounds with short-cropped brunette hair. Renika filled them in on the plan and gave them the information needed to get the job done. With their brief-cases in tow, Amara and Danika walk off in the direction of their mission. Renika walked back to her car and sent a text to the employer, letting them know everything was be-ing taken care of that very moment. They replied with a thumbs up and ace of spades emoji text.

Amara watched out for any unwanted company while Danika picked the lock on the storage container. It took her a matter of ten seconds flat to get it done. Once inside, Amara pulled the door closed and held it while Danika picked the driver side door lock. "Hurry up Danika. The flight is supposed to land in fifteen minutes," Amara said at a whisper.

Danika unscrewed the panel that held the disc player on the dashboard. "Perfection takes time, my friend." she rewired the player with an electronic detonator switch that could be detonated by a wireless device in a two mile ra-dius. "Okay, you're up," Danika said, getting out of the car.

Amara opened her briefcase, pulled out the explosives she wanted to use, and got in the car. She looked at the stopwatch on her Timex. She had three minutes to get it done. *I'm glad I prepare everything*, she thought to herself while placing the explosives inside of the hole where the disc player goes.

Amara plugged the detonator into the jack and flipped the switch to turn it on. "Done," she said and got out.

Danika hurried up and replaced the disc player and screwed it back in place, making it look like it had never been disturbed. Relocking the driver side door from the in-side and locking the storage container back, they walked away from the area coolly. When they made it back to where Renika sat, posted on the hood of her car, Amara stopped the stopwatch. It was a minute until the flight landed.

"Damn!" Amara exclaimed. "Almost perfect," she said, shaking her head. Perfection was one of her affections.

"Aww. Don't beat yourself up over timing, Amara. You're about to be $85,000 to the good in a few minutes," Renika said.

They lounged on the hood of her car, waiting on the flight to land. It came in right on schedule. "Don't you just love Delta Airlines?" Danika said comically, getting a laugh out of her partners.

The airplane came down the runway and slowed to a complete stop. As the passenger's hatch opened, the stairs unfolded to the ground. Thaddeus was the third person in line getting off the flight. In his lime green Armani suit, he walked down the steps without a care in the world.

While he was on the plane, Thaddeus had made up his mind to get in touch with Li'l Will and tell him what was going on. The baggage boy grabbed his luggage and followed him. They reached the storage container, where his car was being kept. It was his travel vehicle that he kept there for purposes like this.

Thaddeus pulled out the set of keys that he had the key to the storage container on. He unlocked the container and stepped inside. "Young man, you can wait right here until I pulled out." He said.

"Yes sir," the baggage boy replied.

Thaddeus unlocked the driver side door and got in. He started the engine and let it run for a minute before driving out of the storage container and stopping beside the baggage boy, who quickly walked around to the trunk and waiting for him to open it. Thaddeus hopped out and popped the trunk for him.

"Nice Audi 8 you have here, mister," he said while putting the luggage in the trunk.

Thaddeus closed the trunk. He stood, admiring the vehicle. "Yeah, it is. I tell you what, if you stick around until I bring it back, it's yours," he promised him.

The young Caucasian male was surprised. "Cool! I'll be here every day!" he happily replied.

Thaddeus hopped behind the wheel and drove off. Renika and her crew were still chilling on the hood of her car when Amara noticed the car.

"That's the mark," she said.

Renika nodded. "Danika, dial him up," she commanded.

Danika pulled out her iPhone, punched in a series of numbers and pressed the call icon. Right before their eyes, the car exploded into flames and rolled out into the intersection, causing a major traffic jam.

"Well, there goes the neighborhood," Renika said before sending the text message to the employer, stating, "*Contract complete.*" "Let's ride, ladies." She hopped off of the hood.

Amara and Danika walked over to the glossy cherry red Phantom and got in with Amara at the wheel. She drove over next to Renika's car and waited until she pulled off. Once Renika hit the gas, Amara tailed her. They rode opposite of the chaos they had caused.

In the rearview mirror, Renika could see the news reporters approach the scene with cameras rolling. She knew the employer had not completed the transaction because they were waiting on the confirmation of the kill. It was only a matter of thirteen minutes after the news went viral that the employer sent her the confirmation of $250,000 had been transferred into Renika's private bank account. She read the text message and smiled, saying to herself, *Justice served.*

Chapter Fourteen

The news of the car explosion at the Dallas, Texas airport was headlining every station as a breaking news report. Machumu and Li'l Will was sitting on the side of the bed eating snow crab, lobster tails, potato wedges and drinking sweet tea from the Olive Garden when the news update interrupted the program they were watching.

"Hmm. This might be interesting." Machumu said and grabbed the television remote, turning up the volume.

The news reporter gave the details of the accident first. When she began talking about the victims who died as a result of the exploded car, pictures flashed on the television screen. None of the victims looked familiar to Machumu or Li'l Will. It was still an interesting story, so they continued to watch and listen.

Finally, the news reporter started talking about the exploded car that caused the fatal car accident. At the mentioning of his name and his picture flashing on the television screen, Li'l Will damn near choked to death on a potato wedge. Machumu patted him on the back until it went down.

"You okay, baby?" she asked still rubbing his back.

Li'l Will coughed a couple times. After drinking half of his cup of sweet tea, he nodded his head. "Yes, baby, I'm good. Dammit, man. What in the fuck is going on around here?" he said.

Before she could answer, her phone started ringing. "Hello?" Machumu answered and said.

"Hi, Machumu! You and Daddy enjoy today's news?" asked the caller. It was Renika.

"What the hell y'all trying to do, start a war?" Machumu asked.

"Consider it blood for blood. At least that is what I like to think of it as being. Not that I really give a damn either way," Renika replied.

Machumu didn't know what to say. She realized that Renika was a woman who played by her own rules and didn't have any sense of loyalty, other than to her crew and the people she considers to be family. She passed her phone to Li'l Will. "I can't with, Renika," she said while shaking her head.

Li'l Will laughed as he answered the phone. "Renika James, what am I supposed to do with your bad ass? What's the move?" asked Li'l Will, still laughing at his wife's sudden change in mood.

"I'm Gucci, old man. The question is, what are you going to do? What side of this coin are you stamped on? Because I can assure you, there's only one winning side," Renika replied with confidence.

"As much as I hate to say it, you're right. I've been loyal to Demetri for a long time. It's fucked up that a good business relationship gotta end like this." He looked over at Machumu, who nodded while giving him the thumbs up.

"I guess we're on the same side of the coin then. Put your wife back on the phone," Renika demanded.

Li'l Will handed Machumu the phone. She sighed, bracing herself for whatever might come out of her husband's daughter's mouth. "What's up?" she said.

"Listen, I need you to contact your Aunty Dominica. Or should I say, Valaire Perfecto Dominica?" Renika replied.

"Either is fine, considering the facts. Go ahead," Machumu said.

"If we are going to keep this big boy business going, we need to get an understanding with your people.

Because, from my understanding, she ain't really with the illegal distribution shit. Well, not the drugs part anyway," Renika stated.

Machumu ate a piece of lobster tail and nodded her head. "You know what you know about Aunt Dominica. I'll see what I can do. But I already know she ain't going for me being anywhere involved with drugs."

"Duh. I'm taking over the empire. Y'all old-ass people can relax, take trips and shit like that. I got this. I'll be the Valaire Perfecto of the illegal transactions," Renika happily replied.

Machumu sighed. "Okay, I'm on it as soon as I can find her phone number."

"Texting it to you now," Renika said while typing Dominica's number into a text message. She sent it to Machumu. "Alright, be about your business, because I'm definitely about mines," she said and hung up.

Machumu opened the text message and copied and paste the number to add to her contacts. Once done, she made the call.

"Hello?" a woman answered.

It had been a long time since Machumu had talked to her aunt. To her, it was almost like a dream. "Yes, this is Machumu speaking. How are -"

"I'm great, Machumu. How are you?" Dominica said after cutting her off.

"Enjoying life, Aunty Dominica. I'm married, we have a daughter. Everything is good," Machumu replied while staring at her husband who was looking at her curiously.

"Machumu, I know you're married to a drug dealer. And you know that shit don't really fly in this family. I don't know what got into y'all after we left home," she said with a lot of anger.

"Well, that's what I'm calling you about, Valaire Perfecto Dominica. I know you wouldn't approve of it, so I have a suggestion," Machumu said hesitantly, hoping for a certain response. And it came.

"I'm listening, Machumu," Dominica said.

Machumu took a deep breath. She knew she had to sell the idea like a perfect salesman in order for her aunt to buy it. "My husband and I are stepping out of the illegal business. It's what his family does, but he's willing to walk away from it. The thing is, his oldest daughter - "

"Renika James. Yes, she and I are very well acquainted. A great business associate," Dominica said after cutting her off again.

Machumu really didn't like being cut short of what she had to say. It was taking everything in her to keep her composure. "A royal pain in the ass is what she is," she replied coldly.

Dominica started laughing. "Oh shit! Sounds like someone has met their evil twin! She's only a pain in the ass because y'all are too much alike!" she said, filled with laughter.

Machumu didn't deny what her aunt said. Truth be told, she was definitely aggravated. "Okay, cool. Are we square on this?" asked Machumu.

"Of course, Machumu, we're straight. As long as your black ass stay away from it and your husband keeps it from around you and the baby, he's allowed to breathe another day," she replied.

Machumu swallowed hard while looking at Li'l Will. She had already come to the conclusion that she would leave certain parts of the conversation out when they talk about it. "Alright then, Aunty Dominica, I'll talk to you later."

"No, you won't talk to me later. Your ass better be on a flight out here the next time I hear your voice. Do you understand me, Machumu?" she said.

"Yes ma'am," answered Machumu before hanging up. She texted Renika a thumbs up emoji before setting the phone on the nightstand.

Li'l Will had placed the extra food back in the carryout bag and set it on the table. When he sat back on the bed, his wife pulled him to her and kissed him passionately before saying, "Now, where were we?"

"Sounds like you were getting your ass chewed out by your aunty," Li'l Will replied.

"Nigga, you better come on with it. I need some compensation for the shit I just went through. Dick, please," Machumu demanded.

"What about the tongue?" he asked playfully.

"Both will do just fine. Come here, baby," she said softly.

They went at it hard until neither had any strength left to continue loving all over the other.

Chapter Fifteen

Demetri had received word of his brother's death. He tried calling Damien and Nicole, but neither answered. Why would they, he thought to himself. He sat the phone down on the bar top and sipped from the glass of Smirnoff sitting in front of him.

By now, he figured, he had no one who he could turn to for assistance besides his own personal crew. The thing about that is, he needed them with him. "Fuck it," he thought out loud. It was better for him to be dead than for him to find out everything and turn against him too, was Demetri's train of thought.

He thought about the people he had been loyal to, although for his own selfish reasons. The one person he felt like he could count on was, Li'l Will, so he called Machumu's phone. She answered immediately.

"What's going on, Demetri? My condolences. Your brother was a great man and an even greater friend," Machumu said.

If he could see through the phone, he would see an I don't give a damn expression written all over her face.

"Thank you, Machumu," he replied sadly. "Is your husband around? I would like to speak with him."

"Sure," she replied. "Hold on," she said before handing Li'l Will the phone.

"Demetri, my heart goes out to your family. A good man died today in a horrible way. Have any idea who would call such a hit?" Li'l Will said, trying to sound concerned.

"No need of trying to chase ghosts, my friend. All I can do is make sure the same ill fate doesn't fall upon me," Demetri replied.

"So, what's this phone call about?" Li'l Will asked, getting to the point. He wasn't good with fake kicking it too long.

"I'm in need of your help. I don't have anyone else who I can trust," answered Demetri.

Li'l Will grunted. He looked at his wife, who eyed him back with a facial expression that said, I'll fuck your world up if you fall weak. Not that he was going to, but the look she gave him reminded him of Renika's words: "There's only one winning side of the coin. What side are you stamped on?" The words were like a ghost haunting his mind.

Li'l Will chuckled nervously. "My man, as much as I hate saying this, fuck you," he said and ended the call.

Machumu gave him a high five. "That's my man!" she exclaimed.

Tired from all of the erotic sex, they fell asleep in each other's arms.

***

Damien had made it to the compound. His first expression matched that of his sister's when she had seen the mansions and the people who lived in them. They were all of African descent. It was like an earthly version of a black Heaven.

They were having a meal with Dominica at a cookout hosted by Josephine. Actually, it was her son's ninth birthday. The grills were pumping, and the aroma of grilled fish and vegetables, fresh coconuts, fig pies, and some of everything else was filling the air. And the food tasted as good as it smelled.

Nicole and Damien were made to feel as though they were at home. They didn't get too many heartwarming smiles, something Josephine had forewarned Nicole about. But it was all love.

The soothing rich sound of reggae filled the air. People danced to the rhythm, some by themselves, while others grabbed partners to enjoy the moment with.

"I see you enjoy the festivity!" Dominica walked up and yelled over the music.

Nicole and Damien both nodded.

"Unfortunately, we have business to discuss! Let's go!" she yelled.

Damien and his sister followed Dominica. The music and joys of laughter and dance faded as they walked down the cobblestone path. It wasn't the same path they had taken to get to Josephine's party, but neither he nor his sister questioned their whereabouts. They figured, if she wanted them dead, that could have been arranged before arrival.

"If you're wondering where we are going, I'm taking you to my private place where I conduct all of such business," Dominica said looking over her left shoulder at Damien.

Neither he nor Nicole spoke a word. They followed Dominica, enjoying the scenery while they walked. They noticed everyone they passed along the way spoke politely to them and asked them to sample food, drink, cologne or perfume. Not wanting seem disrespectful, they accepted the offers.

"Wow! This is nice!" Nicole exclaimed smelling the coconut scented perfume she just sampled. "Where can I purchase a vial?" she asked.

"From the person who asked you to try it," Dominica replied. She knew Nicole would not have understood the old woman because her English was terrible.

"Oh. It's homemade?" Nicole said. She admired the woman for her skills.

"Yes, it is. Everything we just sampled is made by those who offered the samples. They feel it is their way of contributing to the community and it is their own personal business," Dominica replied with a sense of pride.

Nicole nodded. "An Italy version of Black Wall Street. I'm definitely amazed. How much for a vial?"

"$25," answered the old woman. Her English might have been terrible, but she had no problem with giving the price of her merchandise.

"Great. I'll take two, please," Nicole said while reaching into her purse.

Damien reached into his front right pocket. "Make that four. I gotta buy two for Tanji. She - "

"Tanji who?" Dominica asked, cutting him off.

Seeing her facial expression caused Damien to hesitate. He knew the "choose your next words carefully" look from anywhere. "Tanji Harris. My fiancée," he replied.

Dominica shook her head. "I don't think that's a good idea, child. I hope y'all have not slept together yet." Looking at his facial expression, she knew the answer. "What the hell?" she said and threw up her hands.

Damien and Nicole were confused and Dominica knew it. "Your father's name is Noah, right?"

They nodded.

"Noah Sylvan, my Uncle Maceo's son," she stated. She continued shaking her head. "Y'all cousins."

That is what Damien was afraid she was going to say. He dropped his head, staring down at the cobblestones. The cream, dark brown, and ashy grey colors started melding together. "There goes my fucking future plans for a family," he said, sounding upset.

Damien took out his phone and called Tanji. She answered on the first ring, and sounded happy to hear from him. "Hey bae! What's up?" she said.

Damien was at a loss for words. Dominica saw how hard of a time he was having and extended her hand in his direction, saying, "Give me the damn phone, boy. You all tongue tied."

He handed her the phone. "Hello?" Dominica said as she put the phone to her ear with a smirk on her face.

"Who is this?" Tanji asked warily.

"Put my sister on the phone, child," Dominica demanded.

Tanji was a little irritated by the woman's demanding tone. "Who is your sister, ma'am?"

"Ain't your name Tanji Harris?" asked Dominica.

"Yeah. Now who the hell are you?" Tanji shot back defensively.

Her wittiness caused Dominica to laugh. "Gal, you show got your mama's spunk! Put Sarah on the phone!"

Tired of exchanging words with the woman, Tanji called her mother to the phone. "Who is it?" Sarah asked before taking the call.

Tanji shrugged her shoulders. "I don't know. Says she's your sister."

Curious, Sarah took the call. "Sarah speaking. Who is calling?"

Dominica kept her eyes on Damien. He looked like he had lost his best friend. "Sarah Sylvan, how's my little sister?"

The deep island overtone in her voice told it all. "Dominica?" Sarah said hesitantly, not sure if it was truly her.

"Yeah, baby gal, it is I. What in the hell have you allowed my niece to get herself into?" Dominica said.

By the sound of her voice, Sarah could tell whatever it was, it was serious. "Nothing. She is good. Actually, she about to get married."

Dominica started laughing again. Although it was a serious matter, their ignorance of who was who made the matter funny to her. "Nawh, gal, no marry between dem two. Dey kin, gal. Da boy here is Uncle Noah's son boy. How dey gon' marry?" Dominica said.

Sarah damn near dropped the phone. "Ah damn! Dey is kin! Okay gal. Me talk with she now. We on da way dere. We catch early rise flight, gal."

"Okay. See ya soon, baby gal. Loves ya," Dominica said.

"Yes, ole gal, me loves ya too." Sarah said and hung up. Tanji was looking at her, waiting on an explanation. But what she got, she wasn't prepared for. Reverting back to English, Sarah said, "You cannot marry Damien Citural because he is your cousin. He and Nicole are your Great Uncle Maceo's son Noah Sylvan's children."

Tanji's eyes went wide from shock. "You gotta be fucking kidding me!" she said angrily.

"I'm sorry, baby girl." Sarah said as she hugged her daughter. "And that was my sister, Dominica, your aunty, on the phone."

"Well, she could have said that from the jump," Tanji replied coldly.

"Let's finish packing, youngster," her mother said.

They started packing again. While doing so, Tanji thought about how Damien must have felt when he received the same news she just received.

Chapter Sixteen

Teddy and Mike was holding a news conference out front on the steps of City Hall. Their security was beefed up because of the cop killing that was happening at random in Albany. They knew who was behind it, but they had no intention on having them locked up for it. The dead cops families were standing at the front of the crowd, demanding justice be served for the deaths of their husbands, wives, fathers, and mothers.

As Albany's mayor, Teddy took center stage, addressing the matter as best he could with few words. The victims' families weren't letting up on him. They barricaded his mind with not so easily answered questions. Some of which he had no ready answer to or for.

Once they realized Teddy had provided all the information and comfort he could, the families and reporters turned their questions and concerns to Mike. As the sheriff, they expected him to have information on the leads in the ongoing investigation. He stated what he could recall from the statements provided by investigators and public citizens. Other than that, he didn't have much to offer them for comfort or peace.

"People of Albany, especially families of the fallen public servants of Albany, we are going to bring to justice those who are responsible for such heinous crimes! To the victims' families, there will be city assistance offered! Starting tomorrow morning, come down to my office, and there will be a form for you to file in order to get $500 every two weeks for six months to assist with daycare and whatever else you need help with!" Teddy said. His speech soothed over some of the tensions felt from the families.

Teddy and Mike answered a few more questions for the media, and called it a day. They entered Teddy's office, closed and locked the door, and relaxed.

"Fam, I could use a fat-ass blunt of chronic," Teddy said, rubbing his head.

"Hell yeah. Bro, what the fuck is wrong with that nigga? Who he think he is, Fred Hampton of Albany?" Mike asked.

Teddy laughed, shaking his head. "Definitely what shit looking like, fam. My solution to his bullshit is, cutting him out of the game. Let him make his own way. And if he fuck up, let him take his licks."

"Damn, great idea, fam," Mike said. He called Henry.

"Yo, fam, what's popping?" Henry answered the phone and said.

"Dink is on ice as far as touching any work. We ain't got control over what he buys, but he gets nothing handed to him. Understood?" Mike said warningly.

"Say no more, fam. Consider it done," Henry replied. "Aye, my nigga, bounce! We ain't producing that tired-sounding shit!" he yelled at an artist while hanging up the phone.

Overhearing Henry yell at an artist before he hung up had Mike laughing. "Fam, those niggas Henry and T are off the chain with that music shit."

"They must be cussing out another wannabe gangsta rapper," Teddy said.

"Hell yeah. Niggas be knowing they ain't about that life. Talking about jacking and killing. Niggas ain't never witnessed a real jack move. Know their ass soft as marsh-mallows," Mike replied.

"Probably piss and shit themselves if they did, or snitch like a li'l bitch," Teddy added.

They kicked back and cracked jokes about rappers. Neither was trying to be seen in public because they weren't trying to answer any more questions.

***

Sopia and Tanya was serving a breakfast meal on the house for the families of the dead cops. It was something Mike and Teddy had asked them to do, assuring them they would make sure the tab was taken care of. Everything was going great until four masked and heavily armed robbers walked in and started shooting up in the ceiling.

"Y'all motherfuckers know what it is! Break yourself! Throw all ya watches, iPhones, money and valuable shit in the bags! Any sudden moves, and ya ass down bad! Move!" one of the gunmen yelled.

Three of the masked and AK-47-carrying robbers walked around collecting the wealth of the customers. Tanya came walking from the back in a hurry at the sound of gunshots. The order she carried slipped out of her hands upon seeing the masked gunmen. When the dishes hit the floor, the noise spooked one of the gunmen, and he turned around and opened fire.

Tanya's body caught every bullet the automatic rifle released. She was dead before her body hit the floor. Seeing that, the customers started screaming and scattering in panic mode. The masked man who was overseeing the armed robbery panicked and began shooting.

Bodies of men and women were riddled with bullet holes. Sopia had come running out and fell victim to a headshot that splattered brain fragments and blood on the wall. Not a soul survived inside of the restaurant. The gunmen ran out with everything they had collected, jumped in the Dodge Caravan, and fled the scene.

They made it back to their hideout. Quickly, Dink, China, Kaila, and Dolo took off the Dickie jumpsuits and masks. Kaila started a fire in the fireplace and tossed the jumpsuits and masks in it. They watched it burn.

"Man, what the fuck went wrong?" Kaila asked angrily. She was hoping for a clean arm robbery, not a massacre.

"Ain't shit go wrong. We got in and we got out," Dink replied.

Kaila frowned upon his response. "My nigga, we fam and all, but a bitch ain't with killing innocent people just for a few crumbs."

"You think that's what that was about? Them so-called innocent people were the family members of the pigs we offed! And the City of Albany was funding the meals for them motherfuckers! Fuck that! My tax money ain't gonna feed no pig's family!" Dink yelled, defending his actions.

"Whatever, my nigga. We'll get up tomorrow. Let's slide, China," Kaila said. They collected their shares. As they walked out, China threw up the peace sign.

Dolo and Dink was left alone. Dink knew there was a good possibility they would not see or hear from Kaila or China again. While he thought about it and while Dolo rolled up a blunt of Lowd, his phone started vibrating on his hip.

"Yo. Who this?" he answered.

"Seriously, nigga, your ass got issues, bruh!" Teddy yelled through the phone."

Dink held the phone away from his ear with a smirk on his face. *Who the fuck this nigga thinks he talking to?* he thought to himself. He held the phone back up to his left ear. "I ain't got issues, fam. Y'all niggas, you and Mike, are the only two niggas with issues. Y'all niggas supporting the mother fuckers who kill young black teens. Not me."

Teddy laughed, not because he found the shit his brother was saying funny. He was mad as hell. "Yeah? Well, how about this?! I'm personally cutting your ass out of the work! Now, test my G, fam!" he warned him and hung up.

Dink was furious. He punched a hole in the drywall before he knew it. "Fuck!"

"What's up, homie?" asked Dolo.

"Goddamn brother just cut me off. Then he threatened me after the fact, talking about test his G. My nigga, I'm Dink, the first Slaughter Boy. I started this G shyt," Dink stated while beating on his chest.

They smoked the blunt Dolo rolled up and sat around enjoying the high. Dink remembered he had told Mindy he would get up with her and smoke something. "Say, fam, I gotta bounce. We'll get up in a couple of days. Let shit die down." Dink got up and left.

He sat in his ride texting Mindy to see where she was at. She texted him back immediately, letting him know that she was at home. She texted Dink her address, and he hit her back, texting that he was on his way.

Dink swerved over to Mindy's crib and parked on the curb. He jumped out of his ride and trotted up to the front door and knocked. He could hear footsteps approaching.

"What's up, Dink?" Mindy said after opening the door. She was dressed in a Victoria's Secret red panty and bra set with a long flowing open see through top to match. The attire was a compliment to her fiery red hair.

Dink took in her body and fragrance. "Us. Fuck the world."

She giggled girlishly. "Come in." Mindy walked away from the door, leaving it open for him.

Dink walked in and shut the door behind him. Not once did he take his eyes off her nice-sized jiggly booty. He followed her into the den and plopped down on the loveseat next to her. He couldn't keep himself from staring at her, and she knew it.

"What's on your mind, bae?" she asked.

"Wondering if the hair between your thighs is as fiery as the hair on your head. Then again, I'm definitely wondering if the pussy matches it all."

"Let's find out." Mindy said as she came up out of the lingerie.

Dink didn't waste time coming up out of his clothes. They lip locked while touching all over each other. Dink kissed his way down to her medium size breast and sucked on her erect nipples while massaging her breast.

"Mmm, baby," she moaned, relaxing against the armrest of the loveseat.

Dink descended, sliding his tongue down her stomach and into her sex. "Mmm, this pussy tastes like strawberries," he moaned as he tongued her sex down.

Mindy rotated her hips to the rhythm of his tongue. "You like it, baby? You like the way this pussy tastes?" she asked in a sexy tone of voice.

Dink responded by flickering his tongue in and out of her faster.

"Ooh, Dink! Ah! Ah! Ah!" she screamed as she grabbed the back of his head and thrust her hips forward faster and faster until her body trembled. She came.

Dink sucked on her clitoris until she came again. Afterwards, he kissed his way back up her body until his lips met hers. Slowly, he penetrated her, easing himself all the way inside of her. Mindy spread her legs wide and wrapped them around his waist.

She moaned softly as he long stroked slowly. He stared into her sea green eyes and got lost in the moment. "Mindy, damn, baby, you got that bomb," Dink moaned, taking pleasure in the steady rising of heat and wetness between her thighs.

"Yes, baby. I'm glad you like this pussy, because I'm definitely feeling this dick," she replied, staring back into his dark brown eyes.

Feeling his release coming, Dink started stroking harder and faster.

"Yeah! Yeah! Yeah! Fuck me! Fuck me, baby!" Mindy screamed, thrusting herself onto him.

She threw the pussy on Dink so good, he came before he knew it. He kissed her on the lips as he slow grinded inside of her, filling her up with his release. Breathing hard, he got up and sat beside her on the loveseat. He grabbed his pants off the floor, reached inside the right front pocket, and took out a half ounce of marijuana. "You got any blunts, luv?" asked Dink.

"No, but I have some strawberry wraps," she replied.

"Everything in my life gotta taste like you, huh?" he said while licking his lips.

"You'll learn to appreciate it if you stick around," Mindy said before getting up to grab the wraps.

Dink watched her body as she walked out of the den naked. *Walking sex,* he thought to himself. She came back in and sat on his lap. He handed her the Ziploc bag. "Twist it how you feel, luv."

Mindy put a good dime sack in a strawberry wrap and fired up. They smoked and kicked it for a while. Then they went back at it two more rounds. Every time, he came inside of her.

"Dink, baby, you're nutting in me like I'm on the pill or some shit," she said.

Dink hit the weed and nodded in deep thought. "I ain't going anywhere. Whatever we start, I'm there with you to the finish line."

Mindy kissed him on the lips. "I'm holding you to it, bae. Now, blow me a gun."

He blew her a shotgun to the head. She caught all of the smoke. They smoked and sexed each other until they fell asleep naked on the loveseat.

Chapter Seventeen

With everything that was going on, Li'l Will and Machumu decided to go home instead of staying another moment at the Marriott. It was a tough decision because both of them were enjoying being away from everyone else. Especially Machumu. She was thankful for not having to hear a sermon from his mother about whatever she felt was wrong even when nothing was wrong.

When Li'l Will opened the front door, they were greeted by their daughter, Tara, standing with her hands on her hips, frowning. "Daddy, where have you been? I've been calling Mama's phone, and nobody picked up."

Li'l Will started laughing, but his wife didn't find it funny. "Girl, if you don't take your hands off of your hips and stop questioning grown folks about their business, I know something," warned Machumu.

Tara's whole demeanor changed within seconds. Li'l Will picked his daughter up and walked on into the house. "She gonna stop talking to my baby girl like that," he said, trying to cheer her up.

"That's what's wrong with her now," Machumu said coldly. She looked at the time. It was seven minutes after nine. "And why ain't your little spoiled ass in bed?"

"Nana said I could stay up late, and wait for Daddy to come home," Tara replied.

Machumu threw her hands up in defeat and stormed off towards their bedroom. She was tired, and was determined to get some rest. Li'l Will carried Tara up to her room and tucked her in. He kissed her on the forehead and told her goodnight before heading to bed himself.

***

James and DeQuan were tuned in on CNN news. The news of Thaddeus's death was interesting, but not surprising to either of them. You live by the sword, you die in the field, was James's philosophy. DeQuan's theory was, whoever did him in, got the wrong twin. They were really aiming at The Head.

The CNN news reporter stated, after the break, they were going to be live in Albany, Georgia, where cop killings had been on the rise and where there had been a massacre, leaving 98 dead inside of a restaurant.

"What in the hell is going on in Albany, Georgia? Them nigga's gone crazy," DeQuan said.

James nodded in agreement. "You ain't lying. How you gonna have a multi-million dollar scheme and let shit like this go down?" DeQuan asked, referring to their nephews without calling any names because Cedric was sitting behind them.

The news was back from commercial break. They showed footage of the inside of the restaurant while the reporter spoke. Pictures of the deceased popped up on the television screen as he called names and ages. *It had definitely been a massacre,* James thought to himself.

The television and lights went out inside of the cellblock. It was lockdown time. James and DeQuan showed each other brotherly love by dabbing each other up and then hugging.

"Fam, I'll be glad when these last few months come and go." James said.

"Real shit, fam. I never thought I would see it. The Slaughter Boyz out there fucking up heavily," DeQuan replied.

James could feel the emotion in his speech. "I was thinking the same shit, bro. We'll talk in the morning."

Both of them nodded and spoke to Cedric on their way to bed. They knew what he was waiting on.

"Y'all rest peacefully, big bro," Cedric replied. He went inside his cell as well, but didn't lock the door. He waited on the signal from Tiffany for him to come out. The lock on the door clicked twice, and he crept out to the booth.

"What's good, luv?" he asked, kissing her softly upon the lips. He rubbed and kissed her stomach. "And how's our little one doing?"

"We are great, bae. Listen, Cedric, I think we need to chill on this booth thing for a while. You can come out and pick up your package, but after that, you gotta go back in. Besides, we ain't trying to get caught up," Tiffany said.

Cedric nodded. "Baby, you're the captain of this ship. Whatever you say goes. It ain't like we don't talk every day for hours anyway."

She kissed him back on the lips. "Thanks for understanding, bae. We still going to do us every other night. You gotta feed the baby."

They hugged and kissed before she gave him the package and he crept back into the cellblock.

A week passed, and Cedric was back in court on his appeal. Tiffany sat on the row right behind the defense attorney's desk. Every so often, Cedric would look over his shoulder at her. He noticed she was starting to show.

The judge walked in and everybody stood to their feet. After she sat down, she told everyone else to be seated. The bailiff read off the court documents and reason for Cedric's appearance before the court. The judge stared at Cedric during the process.

"Thank you," she said to the bailiff before directing her words to Cedric's attorney. "Is the defense ready to proceed?"

The clean-shaven Caucasian attorney rose to his feet. "Yes, Your Honor, defense is prepared to go forward with the hearing." He replied and sat back down.

The judge turned towards the district attorney. "Is the prosecution ready?" she asked with a warning look in her eyes.

The district attorney stood. "Your Honor, the prosecution is ready."

"Let's get this done before break," the judge said in a tone, making sure both attorneys understood what she really meant. She had a long list of cases on her docket for the day, and she wasn't about to sit through long drawn out appeals.

Cedric's attorney rose to his feet and presented his argument before the court. He argued the insufficiency of the evidence used against his client and the fact that there were no material witnesses putting his client on murder scenes or in drug transactions. His attorney was proving to be worth every cent of the $85,000 he was paid. "The defense asks murder and RICO charges be dropped," he said before having a seat.

While the district attorney stated the nature of the evidence in the case before the court, Cedric smiled from ear to ear. He knew the circumstantial evidence she presented wasn't good enough to hold him in jail. Not to mention, send him to prison. He looked over his shoulder and blew Tiffany a kiss.

All while he was putting on for his baby's mother, he didn't realize Renika was sitting in the back. The smirk on her face said everything. She had witnessed it all.

"The prosecution rests, Your Honor," the district attorney said before returning to her seat. The judge sat quietly, reading over the case and evidence packet before her. "Counselors, approach the bench."

The defense attorney and district attorney approached the bench warily. They argued in a hushed tone before the judge. Cedric was feeling like a free man already. Either they were negotiating a plea deal, or his lawyer was demanding a complete dismissal.

Cedric turned around to say something to Tiffany, but his words got caught in his throat. Renika had changed seats. She was sitting next to Tiffany, smiling.

"What's wrong Cedric? Cat got your tongue?" Renika said without emotion.

Cedric regained his composure before answering. "Nothing is wrong, Renika. Meet my baby's mama and future wife, Tiffany. Tiffany, this is my ex fiancée, Renika James."

The two women were cordial about the situation. They spoke and shook hands. Renika turned her attention back to him. "Glad to see you happy, Cedric Livingston. Have a great life," Renika said in a sincere tone of voice before getting up and leaving.

Tiffany realized she had left her shoulder bag sitting on the pew. She was about to call out to her, but Cedric told her not to worry about it. "Renika James got more damn money than she can spend in a lifetime," he reassured her.

Renika got in on the rear passenger side of the burnt orange 1963 Chevy Impala. Amara was at the wheel and Danika beside her in the front passenger's seat. They listened to the judge's decision concerning the appeal on a listening device planted in the D&G shoulder bag Renika had bought a few minutes ago.

"Well, prosecution, there is no concrete evidence to convict Cedric Livingston of any of the said charges; therefore, I'm granting a dismissal in favor of the - "

Before the judge could get the word defendant out of her mouth, three explosions went off simultaneously inside of the courtroom, killing everyone inside.

"Well, that's that," Renika said with finality. She gave Amara the go ahead to detonate the last round of explosives that she had planted inside the courthouse. They watched as the smoke and fire rose into the sky, burning the building and the dead within it to ashes. Amara pulled off when they heard the sirens in the distance.

***

News traveled fast. James and his brother watched the report on the explosion within the Garland, Texas courthouse, killing everyone inside. They knew it was where Cedric's appeal was being handled. "Karma is a real bitch," James stated.

"Yeah, the li'l nigga had it coming. It's fucked up that his bullshit got a lot people offed," DeQuan replied.

"The price a nigga is willing to pay for thinking with his dick," James said and busted out laughing.

DeQuan laughed as well. "You can say that shit again. Might as well go in his cell and grab the line and pack before the guards get it."

They got up from in front of the news television and sat back at the domino table. James watched the movement in the cellblock and the hallway while DeQuan slipped the lock on Cedric's door and went in. He was in and out in two minutes flat. He took everything to his cell and put it up.

"Everything good," DeQuan said as he sat back down at the table.

Five minutes later, the guards came inside the cellblock yelling lockdown. All the inmates stepped inside of their cells and pulled the doors closed while they packed Cedric's property.

Chapter Eighteen

Mike was sitting at his crib, smoking a blunt to the head, thinking about killing Dink for the restaurant killings when his phone rang, He looked at the caller ID. It was a private number. "Yeah?" he answered.

"Sheriff, how are you doing? This is Demetri."

Mike hit the blunt hard, causing himself to choke on the smoke. "I'm living. What can I do for you?" he asked while coughing.

"How's business?" Demetri asked, ignoring his question.

"Shaky with all the bullshit going on," Mike replied angrily, still considering killing Dink.

"Hmm. Got a shipment coming in for you tonight. Be at the water by nine, and come alone," Demetri said.

Mike hit the blunt again and ducked it out. "Alright then. What's the ticket on it?"

Demetri laughed. "No ticket at all, my friend. This one's on the house. Just consider it a gift for doing good business. Remember, nine o'clock sharp and come alone. Don't be late." He hung up.

Mike tossed the Galaxy S10 on the couch. *Teddy can't seem to control his brother, hell, I might as well get this free money. Fuck 'em.*

Nine o'clock came before he knew it. Mike stood at the edge of the lake smoking a blunt. His thoughts were balanced between memories of Sopia and getting the work and supplying his own crew.

"Psst. Yo, Mike," a man's voice said at a whisper behind him.

Mike turned around. He didn't hear the gunshots, but he felt the hot lead penetrate his chest. The gunman walked up on him and emptied the clip, filling his chest and face with the hot lead that came from the .380 caliber handgun with a silencer to muffle the sound. Afterwards, he took out his cell phone and snapped a couple of pictures of Mike's dead body and sent them via text message to his employer.

"Money being transferred now," the employer texted back.

The contract killer turned his phone off and disappeared in the thickness of the over brush, where his car was hidden. He got in, thinking to himself, *Easy money.*

***

Li'l Will was at the dinner table with his family. His mother blessed the food before they ate. While they were eating, Machumu's phone vibrated on the table. She entered her password to unlock the iPhone. She had a couple incoming multimedia messages and one text message.

She opened the multimedia messages first, and jumped up out of the chair. "What the fuck is this?" she yelled.

Li'l Will got up from the table and ran over to see what was on the phone. When he looked at the pictures of Mike's dead body, he froze. He swallowed hard as he picked up the phone and opened the text message that came from the same number. It read, *"Blood for blood."*

Li'l Will shook his head in disbelief. He called the number. The phone rang three times before he picked up.

"Who the fuck are you, man? Why you fucking with my family?" asked Li'l Will in a tone of voice nobody ever heard him use.

The man laughed maniacally. Li'l Will knew the undertone of the laugh. "Demetri? Demetri, I promise you,

I'm gonna fuck your world up!" he yelled. His family was looking at him with concern.

"Whatever, Li'l Will. Remember, I made you who you are, and I can very well take everything away," Demetri warned him.

"You wanna go to war? My nigga, you got it!" he yelled.

"Your wife knows the game. It's blood for blood." Demetri hung up.

Hands shaking from being in rage, Li'l Will set the phone on the table and walked out of the dining room. He had a loss of appetite. His mind was on murder. *Motherfucker wanna go blood for blood. I'm gonna show this pale bitch.* He grabbed his twin 9 mm, four extra clips, and the prepackaged duffle bag that he kept on standby for situations like this.

Without telling anyone, Li'l Will left through the rear door of the house. He jumped in his 911 Porsche and drove off. He grabbed the throwaway phone he kept in the glove compartment and called and made immediate arrangements for a private flight to Italy.

***

Dominica was rolling over in bed, going into a deep sleep, when her phone rang. Without opening her eyes, she felt around on the bedside table until her hand found the phone. "Hello?" she said, sounding as sleepy as she was.

"Aunty, it's Machumu. I'll be on my way to you on the first morning flight."

Dominica sat up in bed. She could tell something wasn't right. It was all in her niece's voice. "Machumu, gal, what is wrong?"

Machumu gave her the rundown on what had happened. Dominica became wide awake. She listened, and found herself growing angrier by the second. "Okay, gal, come on. If blood is what he wants, he will get it." Dominica hung up. She was so angry, she got out of the bed and walked out onto the balcony. She found a calming peace in staring out over the compound.

"Demetri Citur, I swear to Jah, I'm gonna kill everything breathing with your last name," she swore under her breath while looking up in the starry sky. She gripped the rail of the balcony tight, thinking about Demetri's comment. He was playing the game he knew best. *But a damn fool if you think you gon' win against me,* she thought to herself.

Dominica, finding peace, went back to bed. She slept comfortably, knowing what had to be done and what she was going to do.

Chapter Nineteen

Demetri sat at the mini bar sipping Cognac. He knew Li'l Will was on his way. It didn't bother him much because Italy was his terrain. Something Li'l Will didn't know anything about.

He laughed just thinking about his enemy's foolish moves. It was like a game of chess to Demetri. He didn't consider himself any piece on the board. He saw himself as the hands moving both sides to his advantage.

"Checkmate." He downed the glass of Cognac.

***

Dink cooled it up at Teddy's crib, highly pissed. He knew his brother wasn't playing when he had said he was cutting him out of work, but he didn't think he would go as far as to not sell him any work. He banged on the front door. "Say, Teddy, I know your ass home! Answer the fucking door!" Dink yelled and continued banging.

Teddy opened the door, but Dink wasn't expecting what he did afterwards. He caught Dink square on the left jaw with a hard right cross, causing him to stumble backwards.

"What the fuck?" Dink said, grabbing his jaw.

Teddy had no words for him. He stood on the porch, mugging Dink for a few seconds. He was debating whether or not to go all out on his brother.

"Fam, you ain't even worth it," Teddy said before walking back in his house and slamming the door shut, leaving his brother standing speechless.

"Who was that at the front door?" Teddy's wife asked him when he walked back in the den and sat down.

"Nobody important," he replied while massaging his right hand. *Family just ain't family anymore. Fuck this mayor shit. I gotta get back to what I know,* Teddy thought to himself. He had made up his mind to announce his resignation soon.

Dink realized Teddy wasn't playing around. He jumped back in his car and sped away. He rode through the South Side, contemplating his next move. *Since the nigga ain't fucking with my campaign, I'll take what I want,* he thought to himself as he pulled up on a couple of runners who he knew worked for his brother. He cocked the 9mm and jumped out.

"Assume the position. Y'all niggas know what it is," Dink said calmly.

The hustlers started laughing. "Fam, what the fuck? Dink, don't come around here playing like that!" one of the runners said.

Dink shot him in the left leg, causing him to scream. "Ah shit! Alright, my nigga!"

"Nigga, y'all still think a nigga playing? This Dink, nigga! I don't play! Now, get naked!" Dink demanded.

They came off the few sacks they had left and the money. Keeping an eye on them and a steady aim, Dink collected the goods. Still feeling the pain in his left jaw, he shot both men in the head. He hopped back in his ride and drove off, bobbing his head and bouncing up and down in the seat listening to Spice 1 and 2Pac "Jealous Got Me Strapped".

***

Renika and her crew were lounging around at Danika's spot. They were drinking cranberry vodka and talking trash when the automatic assault rifle gunshots started. Bullets shattered the windows, burying themselves in whatever they made contact with inside of the house. Due to the fact that everyone in Renika's crew were highly trained, they had sense enough to lay down flat on the floor.

"What the hell is going on?" Renika yelled angrily. Her crew never had street beef, so it was odd that someone was shooting up one of their spots. "A bitch must got a death wish fucking with The Squad!"

Renika crawled on her stomach over to the nearest window and eased up on her knees to peep out of the window. Seeing one of the gunmen holding the SKS assault rifle, she ducked back down. "Amara, pass me a mirror! Hurry up!" Renika said.

Amara grabbed her purse, barely avoiding being hit by one of the bullets whizzing through the house at a steady pace. She tossed Renika the mirror.

"I'm gonna show these bitches who's boss around here!" Renika yelled as she cocked the .45 caliber handgun and checked the safety. She held the mirror at an angle where she could see the gunman without having to peer out of the window herself. She aimed a little to the left because she knew the mirror's image would be kind of off and, due to the fact she wasn't in a comfortable position, she knew the recoil would pull the aim perfectly.

Renika took a deep breath and squeezed the trigger twice. Through the mirror, she watched the body drop. The other gunmen, seeing one of their men fall, let off another round and ran.

"Don't run now!" Renika yelled furiously, but to no avail. The shooters were gone. Renika and her crew heard the tires gripping the asphalt as they sped away.

"Who got the nuts to fuck with us?" asked Danika.

"Let's find out," Amara said and walked outside.

It was a good thing that Danika lived in a secluded area, where her nearest neighbor was over a mile away. They dragged the dead man's body into the house and searched him. Renika found a cell phone in the left boot.

"What do we have here?" Renika said, holding the Verizon phone up. She scrolled through the recent phone calls list. There was only one called listed, and she called the number.

The phone rang until the voicemail came on, saying, "You have reached the voice mail box of Demetri Citural. Sorry, but the voice mailbox is full. Please hang up and try your call again later. Goodbye."

"Bingo," Renika said with a smile on her face. "Looks like we have ourselves some work. Somebody wanna shed blood for blood." She used her phone to call Demetri, and he answered immediately.

"Renika James, what a pleasant surprise."

"Yes, it is. How nice of you to send those friendly people over to check on us," she replied sarcastically.

"Nothing too personal, Renika. It's strictly business. I'm tying up loose ends these days."

Renika laughed. "Demetri. Demetri. I got more blood on my hands than I care to think about. Your blood will be just like your brother's. Long forgotten before the explosion happened."

Renika was prepared for war however, whenever, and wherever person wanted to bring it. She had already been given an optional contract for $2,000,000 to off Demetri.

"Fuck the money. This hit is on me," she texted the employer, who responded back immediately with a text saying, Thank you.

To Be Continued...
Slaughter Gang 4
Coming Soon

Willie Slaughter

Submission Guideline

Submit the first three chapters of your completed manuscript to ldpsubmissions@gmail.com, subject line: Your book's title. The manuscript must be in a .doc file and sent as an attachment. Document should be in Times New Roman, double spaced and in size 12 font. Also, provide your synopsis and full contact information. If sending multiple submissions, they must each be in a separate email.

Have a story but no way to send it electronically? You can still submit to LDP/Ca$h Presents. Send in the first three chapters, written or typed, of your completed manuscript to:

LDP: Submissions Dept
Po Box 870494
Mesquite, Tx 75187

DO NOT send original manuscript. Must be a duplicate.

Provide your synopsis and a cover letter containing your full contact information.

Thanks for considering LDP and Ca$h Presents.

Willie Slaughter

Coming Soon from Lock Down Publications/Ca$h Presents

BOW DOWN TO MY GANGSTA

By **Ca$h**

TORN BETWEEN TWO

By **Coffee**

BLOOD STAINS OF A SHOTTA **III**

By **Jamaica**

STEADY MOBBIN **III**

By **Marcellus Allen**

RENEGADE BOYS IV

By Meesha

BLOOD OF A BOSS **VI**

SHADOWS OF THE GAME II

By **Askari**

LOYAL TO THE GAME **IV**

LIFE OF SIN **III**

By **T.J. & Jelissa**

A DOPEBOY'S PRAYER **II**

By **Eddie "Wolf" Lee**

IF LOVING YOU IS WRONG… **III**

By **Jelissa**

TRUE SAVAGE **VII**

By **Chris Green**

BLAST FOR ME **III**

DUFFLE BAG CARTEL **IV**

HEARTLESS GOON **II**

Slaughter Gang 3

By **Ghost**
A HUSTLER'S DECEIT III
KILL ZONE **II**
BAE BELONGS TO ME III
SOUL OF A MONSTER III
By **Aryanna**
THE COST OF LOYALTY **III**
By **Kweli**
A GANGSTER'S SYN III
By **J-Blunt**
KING OF NEW YORK V
RISE TO POWER III
COKE KINGS IV
BORN HEARTLESS II
By **T.J. Edwards**
GORILLAZ IN THE BAY IV
De'Kari
THE STREETS ARE CALLING II
Duquie Wilson
KINGPIN KILLAZ IV
STREET KINGS III
PAID IN BLOOD II
Hood Rich
SINS OF A HUSTLA II
ASAD
TRIGGADALE III
Elijah R. Freeman

Willie Slaughter

KINGZ OF THE GAME IV
Playa Ray
SLAUGHTER GANG IV
RUTHLESS HEART
By Willie Slaughter
THE HEART OF A SAVAGE II
By Jibril Williams
FUK SHYT II
By Blakk Diamond
THE DOPEMAN'S BODYGAURD II
By Tranay Adams
TRAP GOD
By Troublesome
YAYO II
By S. Allen
GHOST MOB
Stilloan Robinson
KINGPIN DREAMS
By Paper Boi Rari
CREAM
By Yolanda Moore

Available Now
RESTRAINING ORDER **I & II**
By **CA$H & Coffee**

LOVE KNOWS NO BOUNDARIES **I II & III**

By **Coffee**

RAISED AS A GOON I, II, III & IV

BRED BY THE SLUMS I, II, III

BLAST FOR ME I & II

ROTTEN TO THE CORE I II III

A BRONX TALE I, II, III

DUFFEL BAG CARTEL I II III

HEARTLESS GOON

A SAVAGE DOPEBOY

HEARTLESS GOON

By **Ghost**

LAY IT DOWN **I & II**

LAST OF A DYING BREED

BLOOD STAINS OF A SHOTTA I & II

By **Jamaica**

LOYAL TO THE GAME

LOYAL TO THE GAME II

LOYAL TO THE GAME III

LIFE OF SIN I, II

By **TJ & Jelissa**

BLOODY COMMAS I & II

SKI MASK CARTEL I II & III

KING OF NEW YORK I II,III IV

RISE TO POWER I II

COKE KINGS I II III

BORN HEARTLESS

By **T.J. Edwards**

IF LOVING HIM IS WRONG…I & II

LOVE ME EVEN WHEN IT HURTS I II III

By **Jelissa**

WHEN THE STREETS CLAP BACK I & II III

By **Jibril Williams**

A DISTINGUISHED THUG STOLE MY HEART I II & III

LOVE SHOULDN'T HURT I II III IV

RENEGADE BOYS I II III

By **Meesha**

A GANGSTER'S CODE I &, II III

A GANGSTER'S SYN II

By J-Blunt

PUSH IT TO THE LIMIT

By **Bre' Hayes**

BLOOD OF A BOSS **I, II, III, IV, V**

SHADOWS OF THE GAME

By **Askari**

THE STREETS BLEED MURDER **I, II & III**

THE HEART OF A GANGSTA I II& III

By **Jerry Jackson**

CUM FOR ME

CUM FOR ME 2

CUM FOR ME 3

CUM FOR ME 4

CUM FOR ME 5

An **LDP Erotica Collaboration**

BRIDE OF A HUSTLA **I II & II**
THE FETTI GIRLS **I, II& III**
CORRUPTED BY A GANGSTA I, II III, IV
BLINDED BY HIS LOVE
By **Destiny Skai**
WHEN A GOOD GIRL GOES BAD
By **Adrienne**
THE COST OF LOYALTY I II
By **Kweli**
A GANGSTER'S REVENGE **I II III & IV**
THE BOSS MAN'S DAUGHTERS
THE BOSS MAN'S DAUGHTERS II
THE BOSSMAN'S DAUGHTERS III
THE BOSSMAN'S DAUGHTERS IV
THE BOSS MAN'S DAUGHTERS **V**
A SAVAGE LOVE **I & II**
BAE BELONGS TO ME I II
A HUSTLER'S DECEIT I, II, III
WHAT BAD BITCHES DO I, II, III
SOUL OF A MONSTER I II
KILL ZONE
By **Aryanna**
A KINGPIN'S AMBITON
A KINGPIN'S AMBITION **II**
I MURDER FOR THE DOUGH
By **Ambitious**
TRUE SAVAGE

TRUE SAVAGE II

TRUE SAVAGE III

TRUE SAVAGE IV

TRUE SAVAGE V

TRUE SAVAGE VI

By **Chris Green**

A DOPEBOY'S PRAYER

By **Eddie "Wolf" Lee**

THE KING CARTEL **I, II & III**

By **Frank Gresham**

THESE NIGGAS AIN'T LOYAL **I, II & III**

By **Nikki Tee**

GANGSTA SHYT **I II &III**

By **CATO**

THE ULTIMATE BETRAYAL

By **Phoenix**

BOSS'N UP **I , II & III**

By **Royal Nicole**

I LOVE YOU TO DEATH

By Destiny J

I RIDE FOR MY HITTA

I STILL RIDE FOR MY HITTA

By **Misty Holt**

LOVE & CHASIN' PAPER

By **Qay Crockett**

TO DIE IN VAIN

SINS OF A HUSTLA

By **ASAD**

BROOKLYN HUSTLAZ

By **Boogsy Morina**

BROOKLYN ON LOCK I & II

By **Sonovia**

GANGSTA CITY

By **Teddy Duke**

A DRUG KING AND HIS DIAMOND I & II III

A DOPEMAN'S RICHES

HER MAN, MINE'S TOO I, II

CASH MONEY HO'S

By Nicole Goosby

TRAPHOUSE KING **I II & III**

KINGPIN KILLAZ I II III

STREET KINGS I II

PAID IN BLOOD

By **Hood Rich**

LIPSTICK KILLAH **I, II, III**

CRIME OF PASSION I & II

By **Mimi**

STEADY MOBBN' **I, II, III**

By **Marcellus Allen**

WHO SHOT YA **I, II, III**

Renta

GORILLAZ IN THE BAY **I II III**

DE'KARI

TRIGGADALE I II

Elijah R. Freeman
GOD BLESS THE TRAPPERS I, II, III
THESE SCANDALOUS STREETS I, II, III
FEAR MY GANGSTA I, II, III
THESE STREETS DON'T LOVE NOBODY I, II
BURY ME A G I, II, III, IV, V
A GANGSTA'S EMPIRE I, II, III, IV
THE DOPEMAN'S BODYGAURD
Tranay Adams
THE STREETS ARE CALLING
Duquie Wilson
MARRIED TO A BOSS… I II III
By Destiny Skai & Chris Green
KINGZ OF THE GAME I II III
Playa Ray
SLAUGHTER GANG I II III
By Willie Slaughter
THE HEART OF A SAVAGE
By Jibril Williams
FUK SHYT
By Blakk Diamond
DON'T F#CK WITH MY HEART I II
By Linnea
ADDICTED TO THE DRAMA I II III
By Jamila
YAYO
By S. Allen

Slaughter Gang 3

Willie Slaughter

BOOKS BY LDP'S CEO, CA$H

TRUST IN NO MAN

TRUST IN NO MAN 2

TRUST IN NO MAN 3

BONDED BY BLOOD

SHORTY GOT A THUG

THUGS CRY

THUGS CRY 2

THUGS CRY 3

TRUST NO BITCH

TRUST NO BITCH 2

TRUST NO BITCH 3

TIL MY CASKET DROPS

RESTRAINING ORDER

RESTRAINING ORDER 2

IN LOVE WITH A CONVICT

Coming Soon

BONDED BY BLOOD 2

BOW DOWN TO MY GANGSTA

Willie Slaughter

www.ingramcontent.com/pod-product-compliance
Lightning Source LLC
Chambersburg PA
CBHW070523260626
47161CB00004B/1619

* 9 7 8 1 9 5 1 0 8 1 3 4 8 *